The Amulet

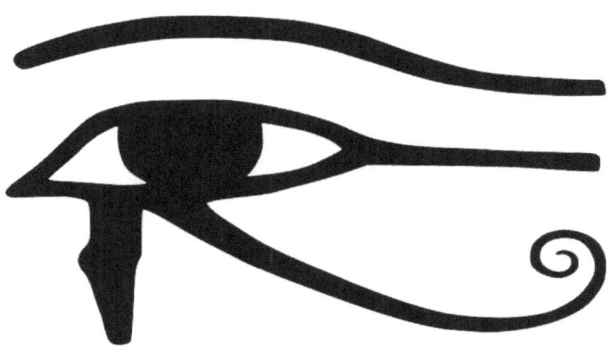

By Sarah Page

No Frills

<<<>>>

Buffalo

Printed in the United States of America

Page, Sarah

The Amulet/ Page- 1st Edition

ISBN: 978-0615665207
1. Amulet – Egyptian – Fiction. 2. Mythology/Fantasy – New Author – No Frills – Fiction.
1. Title

No Frills Buffalo Press
119 Dorchester Buffalo, New York 14213
For More Information Visit Nofrillsbuffalo.com

The Amulet

Glossary

Ab—"Father"
At—"Dad"
Mwt—"Mother"
Wakhashem—"little fool"

Osiris—The Lord of the Dead, he rules over those good souls that make it into the afterlife.
Isis—The Mother Goddess, supposedly the ideal wife and mother; in human mythology, she is wife to Osiris
Set—Twin brother to Osiris; he is the god of deserts, storms, and foreigners, and is often associated with the crocodile

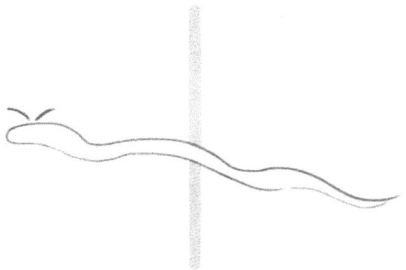

Chapter One

"How did I get into this?" I thought, stirring the tea. Normally, I hate tea; it is expensive and impractical. But this was a special occasion.

I'm sorry, did I say special? I meant completely insane. How many people wake up on their seventeenth birthday and see two feuding gods outside their house? And how many of those would be stupid enough to go outside and scold those gods, who then force themselves upon said stupid person?!

That would be... one person. Me. The genius of Egypt. Usually, I could stop for a few moments, and actually think about what I was doing. But today? Nope. Today I had just suddenly decided to *not* think things through for once and just in time for the gods to show up.

"Are you almost finished in there?" one of the said gods called. He actually looks pretty human... aside from the draconic wings and tail on his body. The Other One is the same way. Except his said extras were black, and the Idiot God's were a whitish-blue color.

"Almost done!" I called back, eager to get them out of my house. I had enough to do without two random gods living in my house. Especially when one of them was this obnoxious creature. I paused and took a deep breath, trying to calm down so that I didn't say something I would regret later. I prayed that they couldn't read minds like the legends said they could.

"Wow, humans are really quite slow," I heard the Idiot God say. I gritted my teeth, trying so hard not to make a retort. I knew that talking back to them would only make them stay longer in my home. Hopefully, he wouldn't be here tonight.

"That is not very nice, at least she is making us tea," the Other One replied. I didn't mind the Other One. He had apologized for fighting, and he had offered to help me make dinner. Idiot God, on the other hand, was rude and pushy, and he presumed far too much.

I finished making the tea, and poured it into my best cups. Which wasn't saying much; they were typical cups for someone of my social standing, made of clay. But it was all I had, so it would have to do for now. Hopefully Idiot God wouldn't make a scene about them being common cups.

"The tea is ready!" I called, walking into the next room. I would call it a living room, but it was also where I ate and slept. My bedroom was currently being rented out to some rich pig. I hated having a man in my small house, especially such an obscene one, but he was willing to pay through the nose to stay here. I actually charged him more than I would charge anyone else, but he also ate a ridiculous amount of food. This was why I made him eat in 'his' room, or outside. The 'living room' was strictly off limits to him, unless he was going through it to leave the house.

The kitchen was off limits to him, too. I didn't really go in there much, either, just because it was so small. I usually only went in there if I had to cook something, or if I needed to get something out of storage. (I didn't have a storage room inside or out, so my kitchen served as both.)

As I walked into the next room, I looked around to see if anything had been broken in my absence. Everything looked okay; the gods were sitting at my miniature table. The two of them looked almost comical trying to fit at it. That table was made for one person, and one person only. I almost laughed.

Before I handed them their tea, I asked, "Are you two ever going to tell me your names? And why were you fighting?" Normally, I wouldn't care, but I was sick of referring to them as 'Idiot God' and 'Other One.' It was a pain.

"Oh, I am sorry!" apologized Other One. "My name is Akori, and this is my brother, Amahté." So they were brothers? That was strange; they hardly looked alike. Perhaps they had different Mwts...? "And we weren't fighting; we were just messing around. We got a bit... carried away."

What? They hadn't been fighting? I shook my head. I guess that being gods didn't excuse them from having 'goofy' fights, just like any boy in Egypt. That...meant that I hadn't needed to interrupt at all. Fantastic.

Now that I could call them by their proper names (although Idiot God was a perfect name for the one called Amahté), I thought that maybe, just maybe, we could have a decent conversation.

And then Idiot God (oh wait, I mean Amahté) decided to open his mouth. "Are you going to give us our tea now?" he asked rudely. "We should get something else, because you took such a ridiculously long time in the kitchen. I thought you had died in there! Why do humans take so long?"

Akori was more polite, just muttering a quick "Thank you" as I handed him his tea. I almost dumped Amahté's tea into his lap, but I reminded myself that all I really wanted was for them to leave me alone. The last thing I needed was some bizarre curse from the gods. So I quietly handed Amahté his tea (even though he didn't deserve it), and stood back, watching the gods have their fun.

How in Ra's name had this happened to me?

The morning had started off so normally; I just wasn't prepared for anything this drastic. Of course, no one could have expected me to be ready for something like this. It had seemed like just another normal day.

I got up early, like I always did, and started making breakfast. It wasn't that hard to make; it was just water with some stale bread and cheese. I ate my breakfast, and generally got ready to go to work. Which was a job as a farmhand. Not exactly the most exciting job in the world. I would rather be a priestess or something, but I certainly wanted to earn my place in the afterlife. And I suppose farmhand is better than slave. For the most part, anyway; I was sure that slaves didn't have to deal with obnoxious gods.

I still don't understand why it had to be right outside *my* house, on *my* birthday. But just as I was about to walk out the door, I happened to look out the window, and there they were. I couldn't exactly ignore them, either. I had to go past them to get to work. If I was late because of them, my pay— one sack of wheat a week—would be cut in half. I couldn't afford that, not right now.

It wasn't like I was asking for a festival or anything on my birthday. I knew that it wasn't that big of a deal. I just wanted it to be a good day, a day where I didn't have to worry about too many things. I was so angry that I couldn't even have something as simple as that, and the next thing I knew, I was walking *towards* them.

"What in Ra's name are you *doing?*" I shouted. I didn't care what they thought of me; I just wanted them to go away, and let me have a good day, a *normal* day. But they must have thought that there was something wrong with me, because Akori's eyes were practically falling out of his head.

Amahté, on the other hand, didn't miss a beat. "What are *you* doing, human?" He sneered the word. "Don't interfere with divine affairs!" He didn't seem like he was truly angry; he just seemed amused. Which pissed me off even more. I mean, if I'm mad at someone, I at least want them to take me seriously.

I should have backed down, but my temper got the better of me. "I don't give a damn about your 'divine affairs!'" I yelled. "Today is supposed to be *my* day. Not yours, not my boss's, mine! And you are *not* going to ruin it for me!" As I finished speaking, Amahté got a huge smirk on his face. Considering the circumstances, I knew that a smirk could not be good—for me, at least.

"Well," he said, "if it's *your* day, then you must have enough time to make us a little treat. You know, to show us that you really deserve it. You came out of this hut right?" He had been walking and talking at the same time, and after he stopped, he ducked inside my house. For a moment, Akori stood next to me, looking back and forth from me to my house. Then his brother called him, and he scurried inside.

And I was left standing in the street, cursing myself and my temper with every foul word I knew. Eventually, I realized that they might start fighting again if I didn't follow, and this time they would be inside my house. With the little that I could afford on a daily basis, I didn't think that I could afford to rebuild or replace everything that I owned.

They had said that I had to make them something, but I wanted them out of my house, fast. I wasn't sure what to make, but then I remembered that I had some tea in the kitchen—a gift from a friend. So I settled on that.

I guess I just answered my own question, though. *That's* how I got into this mess. The two brothers continued to talk, unaware of my mental babbling.

"Thank you for the tea," Akori said softly. "It was

nice." I was starting to understand that he was the only brother with any manners.

Apparently, Amahté didn't agree with his brother's actions. "Don't be such a kiss-up, Akori! She's just a human. I mean, she can see us, but—"

"Of course I can see you! I'm not blind!" I interrupted. Seriously, how stupid did he think I was? He didn't have to be so high-and-mighty, just because he was a god. With the way he acted, I couldn't even think of him as one. That was probably why I wasn't scared out of my mind, considering that I had just told him off.

"Actually," Akori explained, "Most humans cannot see or hear us, unless we choose to appear to them. And Amahté pointed out your sight because we did not want you to see us. Of course, that does not mean that anything is wrong with you, it is just that—"

"Akori, stop!" Amahté yelled, and for once, I was grateful. Something that strange was not what I wanted to deal with. Others couldn't see them? Hmm…maybe my work partner was right about my needing a vacation. Gods or not, I decided to give them a polite push out of my life. I didn't recognize them, so they couldn't be that important or powerful.

"Well…this is getting a little too strange for me. Would you two leave now?" Okay, maybe that wasn't so polite after all. But I *really* wanted them to leave my house.

"Well, actually…" Amahté began. He seemed a bit uncomfortable. Like there was something that he didn't want to tell me. I just waited for him to finish, because now I was really curious. How often did you see a god, let alone a squirmy one? Even if the two of them did seem more like humans than gods. I mean, really. I couldn't let this opportunity pass me by.

He eventually went on. "Akori and I…aren't supposed to be here. Our parents grounded us for 'abusing our flight privileges.' So we can't go back. We would get in even more trouble…" Akori muttered something about it not being his fault at all, and I burst out laughing. I couldn't help it! A god—no, *two* gods—grounded? It was hilarious!

"Of course," he continued, annoyed, "since you're one of the few humans who can see us, that means that we'll have to stay here with you, in your little hut." Well, that sure spoiled it for me. What was I, a farmhand, going to do with a pair of gods?

"First of all," I argued, "this is my *house*, not a hut." I hadn't missed it when he said it the first time. "Secondly, can't you just appear to a prince? Or a priest?! I'm just a farmhand, for Ra's sake! The pharaoh has plenty of family members and priests who could help you."

"Well," Akori said, red-faced, "when we were grounded, our parents bound some of our powers. One of those is sort of our ability to appear to humans. Certain humans—like you—can see us, but we cannot appear. We were by the palace earlier and no one saw us…"

I almost wished that they had lied and pretended to be obnoxious. But now that I knew that they couldn't go anywhere else, how could I turn them away? Even pushy gods deserved a roof over their head, and I got the feeling that if I forced Amahté away, Akori would leave as well.

"Alright," I sighed. "You can stay. But I have to go to work now, so don't destroy the house while I'm gone, and please don't terrorize my neighbors. If they don't see otherwise, they'll blame me." Although I wouldn't mind sending a little punishment Barit's way. She was always borrowing tools and spices from me, and she never returned anything. But her aunt was my boss, so I couldn't tell her no.

I started to leave, but Amahté stopped me. "Work?" he asked. "As in, actual physical labor? I'm going too! I mean, just to watch. I won't touch anything," he added, seeing that I was about to argue.

"Alright," I agreed. I couldn't refuse him; he looked like an excited little kid. And I was already late to work—I couldn't afford to waste time arguing with him. I turned to his brother. "Adori, or whatever your name is, do you want to come too?"

"It's Akori. And I'll stay here, thank you." He was so polite! How could these two really be brothers? Oh, well. At least I only had to deal with one god, even if it was the annoying, disrespectful one. That couldn't be too bad…right?

~*~

"What does this one do?" Amahté asked for the

millionth time. The interrogation was really starting to try my patience, especially since, to everyone else, it looked like I was talking to thin air. At this rate I would be thrown out of town for insanity.

"That's for plowing. Don't touch it, because I actually need it to do my job. Now will you *please* stop talking to me? I can't be seen talking to what everyone else sees as thin air." Despite my request, Amahté continued to chatter away. He was so random; he talked about everything from food to warfare. And he was *so* repetitive.

Eventually, I just decided to try to ignore him. That proved to be easier said than done; Amahté did not appreciate the lack of attention. When he finally accepted that I was not going to respond, he started tripping people with his tail. And who received the resulting death glares? Me, of course. A few people cursed my spirit to eternally wander the earth. (The curses didn't really bother me; I had been 'cursed' to die many times before. After a while, you just get used to it, even if it is annoying.) After someone actually spit in my face, however—which was *so* gross—I lost it.

"For the love of the gods, will you stop it?" I screamed, turning. "You've done nothing but make trouble for me! If you can't control yourself, then get out of my life!"

Of course, Amahté knew who I was talking to, and he hung his head guiltily. But guess who was standing right behind him, thinking that my words were directed at her? My boss. Because the world and the gods were bent on destroying my life today.

My boss' face turned bright red, and I knew what was coming before she said anything. "Fine!" she spat. "There are plenty of slaves willing to do your duty. Don't bother coming back!"

And I had to gather my things and walk out of there with everyone else laughing at my back. Some people even threw things at me!

"Um... Fala?" Amahté began. "I'm really sorry. I didn't mean to—"

"Don't give me any of that crap, Amahté!" I sneered. "I told you to stop. I told you more than once. But you kept going, because you don't need to take orders! I'm done dealing with you! I want you to just keep your mouth shut from now on, got it?!" He nodded miserably, and I almost felt sorry for him.

Then I realized that my former boss would tell everyone that I was a crazy. I would be lucky to find work as a slave now!

Neither of us said anything after that. And as we walked silently home, I couldn't help but wonder: if this was day one, then what would happen in the future?

Oh, dear gods. I was doomed.

Chapter Two

That night, I slept on the floor. Amahté was on the bed, and Akori was on what passed as a couch. Akori had been so great to me; I felt like giving him the bed and making Amahté sleep outside. The fact that Amahté had made me lose my job *and* made everyone think that I was a raving lunatic didn't help to calm that impulse. Akori was the only thing keeping me from throwing Amahté out for the vultures.

Looking back, I realized that I probably should have treated them more respectfully than I had. The old priests would have my head if they knew how I had treated the brothers. Still, no matter how I tried, I couldn't associate those two with figures like Ra, or Horus. They were just…too human. They could be loud or clumsy or shy, just like any human being. But now that both gods were sleeping, it was almost peaceful. And since I could look at them now without any snide comments, I could study their features more closely.

Even without looking at their wings and tails, it was easy to see that they were gods. Both of them were gorgeous. Amahté had fine, dark brown hair that fell into his eyes as he slept. In the back, his hair came down to the base of his neck. Amahté was pretty tall, a good head and shoulders taller than most men, but he was also thin. Under his tunic I could make out a muscular, lithe form. He had a nice tan, but underneath it he was unusually pale, like me.

Akori, on the other hand, had naturally dark skin, and he was shorter than his brother, only about a head taller than me. His hair was shorter, too; it only came down to the base of his head, and it was a sandy brown color. That afternoon, I'd seen that Akori's eyes were a deep gray, while Amahté's were a pure, pure blue.

I sighed. Studying their looks was not helping my self-esteem. I couldn't help wishing that I was even a tiny bit more beautiful to other humans. My skin was far too pale, even with my work tan. My eyes didn't help, either; they were so blue that they were almost violet. No one had eyes like that around here, and no one had my shocking red hair.

My Mwt had always told me otherwise, but I couldn't help wondering if I was the reason that my Ab had left my family. Maybe he had been horrified by my foreign looks, had thought that my Mwt had betrayed him.

Shaking my head, I headed for the door. I needed to get some fresh air.

I ended up sitting on the water fountain in the center of town. Right now it was empty, but in the morning it would be filled with fresh water and gossipy neighbors. Not that I would hear any of that gossip; I was an outcast. It had been that way since my Mwt's death.

I leaned back, thinking. One of the reasons that I was an outcast was my tendency to over think things. I hated the uniformity of this town, and I had spoken out more than once. Nearer to the palace, women were legally equal with men.

But not here. The pharaoh rarely passed this area, and when he did, it was by boat. From the Nile, everything looked as well run as the palace. The problems were within the town structure: with the officials, the tax collectors, and even the priests. To them, the rest of the people were merely flecks of dirt beneath their fingernails. None of them liked a free-thinking individual in their town. According to them, the gods didn't like it either.

But Amahté and Akori didn't seem surprised that I was treating them like humans. In fact, they seemed used to it. When I had first seen them, I hadn't thought that I should respect them because they were gods. I had thought, 'Oh, great. Another fight in front of *my* house.' It was only after they had forced themselves into my house, I had thought that I should maybe be a little more polite.

No matter how hard I tried, I still couldn't put them in the same category as the all-powerful beings that I had learned about as a child. That was probably my Mwt's doing; she had always told me to treat the gods as though they were family figures, and not fearsome beings. I sighed, looking upwards to face the moon. It was a full moon, just the way my Mwt would have liked it.

The moon was especially bright that night. Teanna

looked down and smiled.

"Do you see that, Fala? The moon is shining extra bright, just for your birthday." Her tiny daughter looked back up at her, amazement in her young eyes. And why should she not wonder? She was young; the world had not yet shown her cruelty. 'As it should not,' thought the Mwt, allowing the girl to run ahead.

"Mama," the girl called, "is Atdy watching the moon, too? Is he thinking of me, too?" The woman nodded, not having the heart to dislodge the illusion. Running to catch up to her, Teanna took her hand again, guiding her to the edge of the Nile, where they could watch the stars together.

It was the last celebration that they shared.

I shook my head, willing the suddenly vivid images to fade. Teanna had been my Mwt. I had lived with her, and only her, for the first seven years of my life. Now I lived alone—my boarder didn't count. And I had almost nothing left from my Mwt. Sure, I had other relatives. But none of them wanted to take in a girl who had no past on her Ab's side. That would break their precious tradition, and they certainly didn't want that.

Still, I had managed to fend for myself pretty well. At least I thought so. Other people didn't necessarily agree, but why should I care what they thought? If I saved up enough, I could barter my way out of this prejudiced dump. Of course, now that I had no job that would be slightly difficult...

"Come on, Fala," I told myself, "get ahold of yourself!" I couldn't afford to focus on the negatives. I had to just deal with my problems…starting with the two gods currently living in my house. I stood, pausing for one last moment to look at the moon, and then started walking home.

When I did get back, I found that I was too wound up to actually sleep, so I ended up sitting on the only windowsill in the house. It was really just a little ledge, and it was attached to the only window in the house. When I was younger, I had hurt myself more than once trying to balance on it.

Everything was so quiet. I could see the little mud-brick houses lining the streets, and I could just barely see the well that I knew everyone would congregate around in the morning. The main temple loomed over the town just behind it, and in the moonlight it looked even more impressive. During the day, these streets were crowded and noisy, so noisy that you could barely hear yourself think. But now everything was so peaceful…

"Did I wake you?" a quiet voice asked. I jumped, realizing that I had almost fallen asleep. "I am sorry," Akori continued. "I did not mean to startle you."

"It's fine," I assured him. "I just didn't know you were awake. And no, you didn't wake me up; I couldn't sleep." I was studying his face as I talked, trying to figure out what he was getting at. For most of the day, Akori had seemed pretty reluctant to say anything at all. I wondered why he was talking to me now.

He didn't say anything, though I gave him plenty of time to talk. He seemed like he wanted to have a conversation, but he didn't know where to start. I decided to help him out.

"So," I asked, "is Amahté much older than you?"

He laughed at that; not the response I had been expecting. "Actually, I am older than him. But only by a few minutes."

"You two are twins? Really?!" Twins were such a rare thing in Egypt, and normally one of the infants died or was given away. Most parents couldn't care for two babies at once, especially if they weren't expecting it. Plus these two were just so different—I never would have guessed that they would be twins!!

Akori didn't seem surprised by my reaction. "Yes, we are," he chuckled. "Amahté and I must be even more different than what we think. Everyone we meet thinks that we are years apart."

"Is that why Amahté is so immature?" I asked, my tone bitter. "Because he's younger?"

"Amahté is *not* immature," Akori said, immediately defensive. "He is just shy. Really. To really be himself around someone, he has to get to know them better."

"It doesn't seem like it."

"It is true! Amahté is a wonderful person, and a perfect brother—I do not know what I would do without him. He is so helpful and kind."

I rolled my eyes at him. "Whatever you say, Akori. And I suppose that means he wants to be my best friend or something?"

"...In a way, yes." I stared at him, my face unbelieving. "No, I am being honest! The more he likes someone, the shyer he gets around them. I believe that he likes you a lot; you two would get along."

I turned away from him. A moment passed in silence. Then Akori spoke again, and his voice was pleading.

"He did not mean any harm, you know. It is just... Mwt and Ab do everything for him. He hates being forced to depend on others, and he thought that if he learned to do things for himself, everything would be alright. He really is very sorry." I didn't answer, but I knew that I couldn't pretend to be clueless. He knew that I knew what he was talking about. I still wasn't planning to answer.

Akori saw that and sighed. "Please, just think about what I have said. Amahté is a really great person." Then he turned and went back to his makeshift bed.

As time passed, I began to believe what Akori had said. At first Amahté was not any better. He still mocked me for being human, and he seemed to go out of his way to make things harder for me. He would constantly demand food and leave a mess in his wake that looked like the Nile had flooded my small house. Even my boarder Mtidja noticed.

But after about a week of living with me, Amahté started to improve. He began referring to me by name instead of as 'human', and he didn't purposely leave a mess behind him.

"Fala," he said to me one day, "why is there another man living in that room? And where does he go?"

26

"Ah…that is my boarder. He lives here because it is closer to his farm—that's where he goes every day."

"Why do you let him live here?"

"He gives me quite a bit to stay here. I get half a sack of wheat and two meals worth of meat each week."

"But why do you need that?"

I rolled my eyes. "Because I don't have a job anymore. I need to eat sometime, and last time I checked, so did you and your brother."

"Oh."

That was the longest civil conversation we'd had since we met. Although I felt like he was avoiding speaking with me. I got the impression that he still felt guilty for losing me my job.

Akori continued to come to me almost daily, making a case for his brother's kindness. He told me a lot about both him and Amahté. By the time the second week rolled around, I knew that they both loved flying and playing Senet, even though Akori always won. I knew that Akori's favorite food was pomegranate, and Amahté would eat anything that didn't eat him first.

It was hard to keep them from growing on me. I was learning so much about them—I was the only person who they could talk to, so of course we were going to bond more quickly than normal.

By the third week, I could honestly say that I liked the twins. We were having actual conversations, the three of us, even if I had to be careful of what I said around Amahté.

Every once in a while things would get tense, but I could always count on Akori to diffuse the situation.

The twins were actually helpful, too. Akori was helping me around the house, and Amahté would go on trips to the market. My storage room was running low, though. I was running out of things to barter with. I didn't want to bring it up—I knew it would make things awkward—but I didn't have a choice.

"So...I just wanted to say that tomorrow might be the last day for a while that we get food."

"What? Why?"

"Amahté, we shouldn't pry," Akori said gently.

"Why not? We live here, too."

"Okay, you two," I interrupted. I had never seen the twins fight for real, and I didn't want this to be the first time. "I don't have a lot left to barter with."

"So work for more."

That made me mad. He said it so casually, like it was my fault that I didn't have enough. "Well, I *would*, but I don't have anywhere to work."

My words only seemed to make him mad. "What, and that's my fault?"

"Actually, it is! It's your fault that I don't have a job!"

"Please, don't fight—" Akori began, but his brother cut him off.

"Hey, you were the one who couldn't keep your temper in check!"

"You were the one who couldn't keep your mouth

shut!"

"Ooh, did I upset you?"

"Ra, why are you so stuck-up? Go drown in the Nile you jerk!"

"Oh, go run to your Mwt—wait, you don't have one. What, did she abandon you?"

I stared at him for a moment, dumbfounded. Then I drew my hand away and backhanded him as hard as I could. "How *dare* you bring my Mwt into this," I spat.

He opened his mouth to say something else, but I didn't wait to hear it. I just turned and walked away from him without a word, ignoring Akori's apologies.

I walked for the rest of the day, my anger fueling me. How could he say that? He didn't know that my Mwt was dead, that was true, but what right did he have to say that?

Gods, how could I have thought that we were getting along?

When I finally returned home, I had made my decision. Akori could stay if he wanted to, but Amahté simply had to go. He wasn't there when I got back, but Akori was waiting for me.

"Fala, can I talk to you?"

"I'm sorry, Akori, but your brother has to leave. He can find somewhere else to stay."

"Please, Fala, he is so very sorry, he did not mean to upset you."

I turned sharply to face him. "Stop *lying* for him, Akori. He meant every word he said. He—"

"No, Fala! I am not lying for him!" I stared at him for a moment. Akori was always so quiet and polite. If he was so worked up over this…then the least I could do was let him finish speaking. "Amahté has a quick temper. I will not deny that. But he would never, *never* intentionally hurt someone that way. Mwt and Ab…the way they treat him leads to a lot of horrible things.

"And since I am not the one to inherit the estate, I get treated even worse. Amahté has seen me hurt too many times to ever want to do that to another person. He went on a flight so that he could calm down so you two could talk. I am not asking you to forgive him. I am simply asking you to give him one more chance."

I sighed. "I…I'll think about it. But I can't promise anything."

He looked relieved. "That is all I am asking for, Fala."

Breakfast the next day was awkward, to say the least. Amahté didn't say a word, and instead sat staring at his food. Akori took the same approach, glancing between Amahté and me, his eyes pleading.

Stupid guilt reflex.

"So," I began with unnecessary cheer, "how did you two sleep last night?" All I got for my effort was a pair of mute nods. I hadn't even asked a yes or no question! They were gods, they should be able to pull themselves together better than this.

I decided that the saying 'desperate times call for desperate measures' fit here perfectly. I had thought about what Akori had said, and he was right. I couldn't criticize Amahté for having a short temper when I had one just as short—he deserved one more chance. "Amahté, I have to run some errands. Do you want to go with me?" I was probably going overboard, but I wasn't sure what else I could do. Akori, at least, seemed to appreciate my effort.

"I...I guess I'll go. Sure," he answered, confused. We stood. "Where exactly are we going?"

"Just to the market. I have to get some food, what with you two eating like there's no tomorrow." I glared at the brothers. "You two really do need to stop that. You're going to eat me out of my house!!" They just grinned sheepishly.

I stopped briefly to grab what little I had to barter with. I would be better off getting more than I needed today—it might be a very long while before I could get food again.

As we left the house, I told Amahté, "You had better thank your brother. He's the only one who thinks that you can actually be mature."

"I know," he whispered. "He's much more loyal than I deserve." We walked in silence after that. I didn't know about Amahté, but I just didn't want anyone else thinking that I was a lunatic—or worse, a demon sent by Set. Along these streets, there were only the small children and the sick left behind in the houses. Sometimes we passed a man on his way to work or a woman on her way to the market, and each time we acknowledged each other with a simple nod.

I liked to walk around town, but I hated walking to the

market. My house was a lower-end one, so to get there I had to walk through the poorest section of the town, the part filled with cripples, orphans, and lepers. It made me uneasy to see them. Most of them were stark naked—they couldn't afford food, let alone clothes—and they were always filthy. But the worst part was their eyes. You could see the hopelessness and despair with just one look.

When we got through that, I always breathed a sigh of relief. When I'd had more, I would usually give out some wheat or a loaf of bread. I couldn't afford that now.

Once we got to the market, we could actually talk. The buzz of gossip was so loud; no one would notice me talking quietly 'to myself.'

Today was a bad day for shopping. The merchants were overpriced on everything, and half the merchandise was bordering on rotten. But I needed to get food. All I could do was try to haggle the price down and try to pick the best deals. Still, more than half of what I had to barter with was gone before I knew it. I needed food, but at this rate my wages would last me less than a week.

The decisions became harder as my wheat sack grew lighter. Should I keep some wheat and use it to pay for bread? Or should I pay this man the ridiculous price he was asking for some meat? While I was deciding, I would almost unconsciously finger my Mwt's necklace. Amahté noticed, and his curiosity finally got the better of him.

"Why do you keep doing that? It's not like it's going to help you make decisions or anything."

"I know that. But it belonged to my Mwt; she gave it to me just before she died."

I could tell that my response caught him off guard. "I... I'm sorry... I thought that she was just... I don't know, away with your Ab or something."

I shrugged. "I don't really have an Ab. He left before I was born." I said this all coolly; there was no sense in bringing up old grief.

"Oh." He pointed to a nearby vegetable stand. "Why do we need this?" I held my breath and counted to ten before answering. I knew that he was just trying to be polite, but sudden topic changes had always annoyed me.

"*You* probably don't. But humans, such as myself, need nourishment, and that's what these are for."

"Oh...how much more shopping do you have to do?"

"That was the last thing I needed. We can go now." I actually needed to buy a few more things, but I could come back for those. I could tell that Amahté was getting bored. And I didn't think that I could fit any more food in my bag.

Just then, a man ran by us, nearly knocking me over. Normally, I would have ignored it—people can be just plain rude—but he had taken my Mwt's necklace with him. I started to run after him, but Amahté grabbed my arm.

"Where are you going?" he asked. "You didn't see his face, and he got a head start. You'll never catch him on foot."

"What other way is there?" I spat, aggravated. "Are you going to pull a chariot out of your tunic?"

"No," he said mischievously, "but we can always go my

way." His grin almost made me not want to follow the thief…almost. I nodded, praying that 'his way' wouldn't get me killed. Laughing, he scooped me up in his arms, despite my protests. I was about to ask how this was going to help when he took off.

Now, I had never been any higher than the top of my one-story house. So when I looked down from my perch in his arms, it was the first chance I had ever had to realize that I was afraid of heights. My fear must have shown on my face, because Amahté laughed again and flew closer to the ground. Or maybe he just saw that I was practically crushing the food sack in my arms.

I was trying desperately not to vomit when I realized something. "How is this going to help? We can't see anything from up here; how will we find him?"

"Correction: *you* can't see him," he told me. "My eyesight is far better than yours. Oh, there he is. Hang on!" I held on tight as Amahté went into a steep dive. We landed right in front of the worthless thief who had stolen my necklace. For some reason, his eyes were practically falling out of his head. If I hadn't been so scared from my little flight, I would have laughed. As it was, I was extremely pissed.

"Give back my necklace!" I snarled. He hesitated for a moment, then shook his head and turned to run. I supposed I didn't look very threatening—my hair was mussed up from the wind, and I was still carrying my things from the market.

Amahté was already behind him, though, so he didn't get very far; the loser tripped over Amahté's tail.

Now looking completely panicked, he scrambled forward, leaving my necklace in the sand. He was somehow running before he was standing up. Amahté pushed him once more, and for once, I didn't mind.

Once he was gone, I muttered, "What was wrong with him? He looked terrified."

"...Fala? Remember what I said about most humans not being able to see me?" It took a moment for me to understand what he meant. Then I got it: to everyone else, it must have looked like *I* was the one flying. That might be a little hard to explain to people. Oh, well. At this point, I was half-expecting the pharaoh himself to come and lock me away. I wondered if *he* would believe me about the twin gods...probably not. I shook my head, dropping my sack and walking over to reclaim my necklace.

It wasn't very big; the necklace was about the size of an egg. In the center was a sapphire, gold-plated around the edges. The back was also gold-plated, and the chain was solid gold. Delicate designs covered the gold, but there wasn't a single mark on the sapphire.

It was small, and I wasn't even sure if the jewels were real. But that was okay. I didn't mind. I picked it up, brushing away the sand.

Amahté chose *then* to talk. "So...you're afraid of heights, Fala?"

"Shut up!" I retorted. "It's not like you gave me any warning. You just picked me up and...and...flew!!"

"Okay, I'll give you a warning next time. Maybe you'll

fare better," he teased. "I don't see how it could get any worse; you look like you're about to vomit!"

I groaned. Not only because he had said 'next time,' but also because that next time was now. Wherever we were, I didn't know how to get back to the market on foot.

"Hey," Amahté said, interrupting my thoughts, "may I see this all-important necklace? Or is that off limits?"

"You can see it. Just be careful; if you break it, you're dead." He held up his hands in surrender, and I handed him the necklace.

"Fala?" he said softly. "I am glad that we got your Mwt's necklace…and I'm sorry that I said that about your Mwt yesterday."

"It's alright, Amahté." He smiled at me, and turned his attention back to the necklace. I thought that he would just look it over, then toss it back. Instead, he tensed up and the smile vanished. "Amahté? What's wrong?" I asked. To no response. "Amahté?"

"Fala…can I borrow this for a while? I know that it's important to you, but…" He wasn't really asking, though. From the way he said it, I could tell that it was more of a demand. I didn't want to give it up; it was from my Mwt, and it was the only thing that I had carried around with me. But he *was* living under my roof…I could always take it back.

I nodded, praying that this wasn't some kind of twisted joke. He pocketed my necklace and held out his arms to me. He knew that I couldn't get home without him. I grabbed my sack and let him pick me up; at this point, I just wanted to get home. But I still didn't understand his reaction to my necklace, and he didn't bother to explain it.

We landed just outside of town. From there, we went on foot; I didn't want anyone else to see me 'flying.' I, for one, was happy to be back on the ground. Amahté was just really, really serious. To be honest, it was kind of scaring me; I hadn't thought that he could be so intense.

He didn't say a word, not even after we got home. And when Akori asked, he just shook his head in response. So the house was unnaturally quiet for the rest of the day. Just before dinnertime, Amahté pulled Akori aside. I could hear them talking from the other room, but I couldn't quite make out what they were saying. I assumed that it was about my necklace, though; Akori came out looking just as serious as Amahté.

The two of them went on like that for a full week. They were ridiculously elusive, and when I *did* manage to talk to one of them, they would keep the conversation as far away from my necklace as possible. If I managed to bring it up, they would change the subject.

At the end of the week, I had to go shopping again. Thanks to my luck, the prices were just as bad as when I had gone with Amahté. I only ended up getting some fruit, and planned to go again the next day. Then I headed home. The house *would* have been peaceful if it wasn't so eerie, as it had been for the past week. It was almost dead silent…at least until just before dinnertime. My boarder, Mtidja, decided to move his fat, ugly self into my living room.

"Girl, I demand to know what's going on!" That's what he always called me: girl. I don't think he knew my name, even though he'd been renting a part of my house for almost a year now.

I tried my best to be polite, hoping that he would just get bored and leave. "Um...I'm sorry, but I'm not sure what you're talking about." Which was true; I had *no idea* what he meant.

"Don't play *dumb*, girl. I haven't been getting as much food lately. And I hear you *talking* to yourself sometimes." He looked at me with revulsion.

"Oh, that. That's just because I didn't have as much food in the kitchen as I usually do," I told him. Also true. "But I went shopping today, and I'm going again tomorrow." No need to tell him that tomorrow would be the third time in a week that I had had to go shopping.

His eyes narrowed, and not for the first time, he reminded me of a pig. "Why would you need to go shopping two days in a row?"

"None of the affordable merchants were there today. They should be back tomorrow."

Mtidja lumbered towards me, and I had to fight the urge to cringe back. His eyes scanned the room, finally resting on my collarbone, where my Mwt's necklace usually was. "...Where's that necklace of yours?"

I scrambled to find an excuse. "I...I took it off. I didn't want it to get stolen at the market, and I...haven't had a chance to put it back on yet."

"Why not?"

"Er…I've been…cleaning." He took a step back; he seemed to be thinking. I had to fight the urge to gasp in the now fresh air. What would I tell him if he kept asking? I could only keep this a secret for so long—he *was* living here.

"Do you want me to stay here?" he asked.

No, I didn't, not at all. I would much rather just have him leave. Then I could have my house back… But right now, he was my only source of income, so I said "Yes."

"I want…that pretty little necklace of yours, and you will be my slave." I gawked at him. "You heard me, girl. I'm not stupid; I know what's going on. You lost your job. Without me, you would have no money. You'll end up on the streets, and no one will help you because everyone knows you're going crazy and you have no heritage. You have no chance. Gimme the necklace now, and agree to be my slave; maybe then you'll have some worth in this life."

I was about to tell him that there was *no freaking way* that I would *ever* do that…when Amahté put his hand on my shoulder. I jumped; I hadn't expected him to intervene.

"Fala, tell him you'll—"

"Shh!" I hissed. What was Amahté thinking? "Um, I'm thinking," I told Mtidja.

Amahté waved it off. "He can't hear me, Fala, don't panic." Oh, that's right. I kept forgetting about that. "Tell him you'll give him four rubies, a diamond, and an onyx stone." My disbelief must have shown on my face, because he said, "Don't worry, I've got it covered. Just tell him."

"Um…I'll give you…four rubies…a diamond and an onyx stone if you leave?" Mtidja's face lit up at this; it must have been more than he was hoping for. Amahté moved my hand behind my back and handed me a small knapsack.

"Hand them over!" the pig commanded. I gave him the bag, which he practically tore the top off of. After looking over the contents, he headed for the door. "I was planning on leaving anyway," he called over his shoulder. "My servants cleared my things out yesterday while you were gone." And with that, he was gone.

I turned on Amahté. "What in the name of Anubis was that?"

He shrugged, looking not the least bit sheepish. "That was me helping you. I figured that you glaring death at him meant that you wanted him gone, so I got rid of him."

"No, I mean with the jewels! I've been worrying my butt off constantly, trying to figure out how I was going to afford the things I need *without a job*—" I glared at him— "and you can manage to *throw away* jewels?! Why didn't you tell me?"

"I didn't think that you would want to accept things from me. You have always seemed like the type of person who wanted to make it on their own."

"Normally, yes, but I'm not just taking care of myself. I have to take care of myself and both of you, and I now have no source of income."

"Oh. Well, I've got some more, if you want them. They're a pain to lug around, anyway." He said it so nonchalantly!

I just shook my head. "Whatever. I'm just going to go make dinner and...try to stop being surprised by you and your brother." I walked towards the kitchen, but Amahté ran in before me.

"Don't worry about it," he said. "I can cook. Or...I can get ingredients while Akori cooks." Before I could protest, Amahté was dragging me over to the couch. "Um, are you okay? That pig didn't hurt you, did he?" I laughed at his face; he was honestly worried! "What is it?" he demanded.

"It's nothing," I giggled. "He didn't hurt me. He couldn't if he tried; he would find a way to punch himself in the face or something. And, anyway, I know how to fight if I have to."

The worry on his face faded, only to be replaced with confusion. "Alright, but...it's not that funny."

"I'm not laughing at that," I said, finally getting myself under control. "I just thought that *you* were kind of funny. You and Akori have been quiet and serious all week and all of a sudden you're panicking. I'm glad; you're kind of frightening when you're serious." He opened his mouth to say something, but I cut him off. "Speaking of being serious, what's going on? Why are you so interested in my necklace all of a sudden?"

"...I don't know if I can tell you."

"Come on, Amahté, I think I deserve to know!"

He took a deep breath. "You're right. Okay, I'll tell you, but..." He blushed. "I really don't think you're going to like it."

"How can you be so sure?"

41

"Oh, trust me, I am quite sure on this one."

I waited for a moment, but when he just continued to look at me nervously I said, "Are you going to tell me or not?"

"Oh, right!" I rolled my eyes. How was he going to do *anything* with his life with that attention span? "Well, you know who Osiris is, right?" I rolled my eyes at him; of course I knew. Everyone in Egypt knew that Osiris was Lord of the Dead. "No need to get snippy! It's important, you know!"

"Important *how*, Amahté? Please just get to the point." At this rate, I would be better off finding the answers I wanted on my own.

"Er...Lord Osiris had a wife who was forced to live in the human world because he is a High God and not a regular god. He made her an amulet, which was stolen before Akori and I were born, even before he could give his wife her gift."

"I didn't know that there were different classes of gods."

"Oh, yeah. There are a whole bunch of different classes. High God is the highest class, but there are only thirteen of those, with Ra at the top. Then comes god, then middle god, also called demi-god. The lowest class consists of beings that aren't even considered gods; they're called godlings." He rolled his eyes. "Most of them don't even live in our realm—they live among the humans. But if one person in the family gets elevated to a higher class, then the whole family moves up."

I struggled to understand what he was saying. "How...How do the High Gods decide which class you're in?

And how do you move up?"

"It's just based on the amount of power and ability you have, and how well you can use it. If you get more powerful, or you learn to better control your power, then you have a chance to move up. Most of us don't, though—we are mostly happy where we are. So anyway, about your necklace…"

I did not like where this was going, not one bit.

"Our parents have told us what it looked like and what it feels like—"

"Feels like? What does that mean?" I was fairly sure that a necklace would feel like, you know, metal.

"You keep interrupting me! Do you want to hear the rest or not?" I nodded, and he continued, "I mean how its *aura* feels. Everything has a particular aura to it, whether it's alive or not. We've been taught to keep a lookout and…I am fairly positive that this is it."

I stared for a moment. "How come no human knows about any of this? And why is Isis in the human world?"

"Isis and Osiris are just together for show, and only in the human world; we don't know who his real wife is. Have you ever noticed how Osiris and Isis look kind of cold towards each other, even in their statues? Well, that's why. And do you really think that humans could wrap their mind around this?"

I thought about that. Some humans would, but anyone in a position of power would deny it. I remembered that, as a girl, I had asked a priest if child gods liked to play ball. The man had nearly branded me as a hypocrite and a 'threat to the gods.' And asking about how gods met got me banished from the religious school that my Mwt had tried to send me to.

I shook my head and sighed. "How could this have happened?"

Amahté shifted uncomfortably. "I'm not sure how it happened, but…your Mwt's necklace *is* the Osiris amulet." Seeing that I was about to protest, he added, "There's no mistaking it. A copy wouldn't have this kind of magical aura; it's way too powerful to be anything else."

I sagged back against the couch. *I* was in possession of a divine item. "Wait, why did you just notice? I wear it everywhere, and neither of you said anything before."

"We aren't very good at reading auras yet. It takes a lot of training to read auras without touching things, training that we don't have."

"You've bumped into me plenty of times before."

He rolled his eyes. "But that's *you*. Not the amulet. We could sense that something was a bit off, but we thought that it was you. You can see us, after all, and that's unusual in its own right."

"Oh…" What was I going to do now? I knew what I *should* do: give up the amulet so that the twins could find its proper owner. No matter who it had belonged to before, it had also been my Mwt's, and it was mine now. I didn't want to give up something that had been so dear to my Mwt's heart.

"I'm sorry Fala, but I have to ask…where did you get that?"

I hesitated before answering. What if he thought I was guilty of stealing it? Or worse, if he thought my Mwt was the guilty one? "I asked my Mwt where she got it once. She said that it had been a wedding gift from my Ab. I know that my Mwt would never steal it, she would never steal anything."

"If that's the case, then my guess is that some merchant had it," he told me. "Your Ab saw it, thought it would be a good gift, and bought it for your Mwt."

"And it got stolen…by the merchant?"

He shook his head. "Probably not. Whatever or whoever stole it probably wanted to get rid of it to avoid being punished by Lord Osiris. It must have just recently made it into the hands of the merchant."

"How is that possible? From the way you were talking about this, it happened a long time ago. Wouldn't the amulet have gotten back to Osiris by then?"

"No, not necessarily. While Osiris and his wife were together, the woman's aging process was slowed, since gods live much longer than humans. If the woman is still alive, she would be over eighty years old, but she might not look a day over thirty. And in the human world, it's easy for things to get lost."

Akori entered the room just then. He took one look at me, then turned to Amahté. "I thought that you were not going to tell her."

"Wait, why weren't you going to tell me?" True, they had been secretive about it, but I hadn't thought that they were going to keep it from me forever. The brothers exchanged glances, and I could tell that they hadn't planned on answering this.

"Well…" Akori began, "the Osiris amulet belongs to his wife and his daughter—whose names we do not know. It is too powerful to entrust to anyone but them, so we need to find out who they are and how we can get it to them."

Amahté took over. "However, Akori and I can't tell who originally had this. Whoever wears it leaves a sort of trace, but because you've been wearing it for so long, Osiris's wife's trace is blocked. Our parents could probably read it, though."

He didn't say anymore, but he didn't really have to. "So," I continued for him, "you were going to leave, and take the amulet back to your parents. Without telling me." They nodded miserably. "Are you still going to take it?" More nodding. "Fine. But I'm going with you."

"What? You can't—"

"Oh, yes I can," I insisted. "Osiris amulet or not, I got that from my Mwt. I'm not giving it up until we find out who it rightfully belongs to." If I had to hand it over, then I was going to make sure that it went to the right person.

Akori interjected on my behalf. "Fala has a point, Amahté. Also, because she gained the amulet through inheritance and not just as a gift, it will offer her some protection."

"…Alright," Amahté conceded. "You can come. You don't have to bring any clothes, because we have plenty of extras at our estate. Only bring something if it's irreplaceable to you."

It turned out that the only thing I needed to bring was the amulet. My Mwt's dress and letter were too precious; I was afraid that I would lose them. Amahté and Akori put a simple barrier around them that they assured me would deflect anyone who tried to steal them. That was good, because it made for light traveling. However, that also meant that I was light enough to carry, so we would be flying. Which was bad. For me, at least; Amahté and Akori were thrilled that they would get to stretch their wings.

We set off, my Mwt's necklace once again placed around my neck.

Amahté said, "Okay, the first thing we have to do is, obviously, find you a room. Then you can meet our parents! I think you'll really like our Mwt." I noticed that he didn't mention his Ab, but that was okay. I could take this one god at a time.

Even though the flight was long, it wasn't so bad. Maybe because this time I had gotten a warning. Actually, I kind of enjoyed it, but I would never admit that to Amahté. Akori, maybe, but not Amahté.

After a while, I started to get pretty tired. I hadn't been sleeping well; I had been so worried about my Mwt's necklace. But now that I knew what was going on, I was exhausted. I drifted off long before we reached our destination.

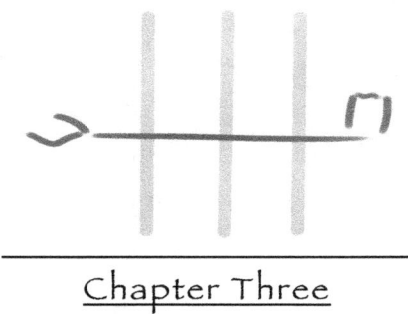

Chapter Three

The first thing that I noticed was the smell. Or, more accurately, the lack thereof. It smelled so *clean*.

The next thing that registered was the bed; it was way too soft to be mine. For a moment, I thought that I was still dreaming. What other explanation could there be? I didn't move. I wanted this dream to last. Then I remembered the events of the previous day…I remembered where I was. I was at the twins' estate. I decided to open my eyes and see where they had put me.

Maybe I wasn't awake just yet, because the room before me just couldn't be real. For one thing, the bed that I was in was big enough for at least five people. I couldn't understand why it had to be so big; didn't gods have a sense of practicality?

There was translucent violet fabric surrounding the bed. The covers were a light, almost delicate lavender color. They were so soft…they were probably made of silk. Through the canopy, I could see that the room contained a dresser (with a mirror mounted on top of it) and a wardrobe. Closer to the bed, there was a full-length mirror. It looked like gods enjoyed admiring themselves. Next to the dresser (across from the bed) there was a door leading into the washroom. On my right, opposite the mirror, was a closed door that most likely led into the hallway.

Reluctantly, I got out of bed and went to the wardrobe. Inside, there were only dresses; the other clothing was probably in the dresser. The dresses were so simple, which I was grateful for, but they were still so…different from what I was used to. These had poofs and bunches in strange places. I was sure that even the pharaoh's wife didn't wear things this overdone.

Although I might not have much of a choice. It was *cold* here. A breeze blew through the window, and I shivered. At home, it got pretty chilly during the night, but in daytime it was warm enough to go without any clothing at all. Here, not so much apparently.

I was standing there, trying to decide whether the warmth would be worth the discomfort when I was startled by a knock on the door.

"Um…Come in?" I called uncertainly. I didn't want to be overly polite, in case it was nothing, but I didn't want to be rude, either—it might be someone important.

"Hello, Fala. Are you truly awake this time?" a voice teased. I relaxed. It was only the twins. Akori looked happy to see me; Amahté just looked like he wanted to disappear.

"What do you mean by 'actually awake,' Akori?" Now that Amahté could clearly see that I was awake, he chose that moment to duck out of the room. I ignored him—he was probably just having one of his weird moods again.

"There were a few times when we came in to check on you and you began talking in your sleep. It was interesting, to say the least. Does it happen often?"

I was so horrified that I couldn't answer. I knew that I talked in my sleep. It usually happened whenever I felt too strained, or when I felt guilty. With only my boarder in the other room, it had never been a problem. And usually, I only revealed small things, things that weren't important. However, with how extreme the past few days had been, I didn't doubt that I may have told them quite a few things that were...well, embarrassing, to say the least.

"What did I say?" I finally managed to croak.

Akori laughed at my worry. "Do not panic; most of it was not new. You mostly spoke of small worries, like taking care of your home. Ah...I really am sorry about your Mwt, though. I just thought that she was away on some kind of business." I accepted his apology with a small nod, surprised that Amahté hadn't told him.

"You said *most* of it was old," I realized. "What else did I say?" Akori wasn't laughing anymore. Now he looked slightly embarrassed.

"You did talk about Amahté and me a bit. And. . . ." he hesitated.

"And? Please tell me, Akori; I deserve to know!"

"Well...there was a lot about us, as I said. Some of it really is not fit to repeat..." At that, my face burned, but Akori continued. "That is why he left. He feels as though he needs to leave you alone for a bit. He is simply shy." Akori had told me this before, but I still wasn't sure if I could believe him. Amahté just didn't seem like the 'shy' type of person.

"Actually," he continued, "I think that he really enjoys your company; perhaps you could talk to him about this. I am sure you two would make each other happy. Or at least make each other feel less…awkward."

"I get it, Akori," I sighed. "Maybe while I do that, you should practice being subtle. You all but spelled out what you want me to do." He grinned, and his expression reminded me of Amahté. Then he left the room.

Of course, I wasn't going to talk to Amahté. At least not in the way that Akori wanted me to. I would rather be at the bottom of the Nile being attacked by crocodiles than talk to Amahté that way. I suppose that most young women would love to have a chance to be with him, but I was *not* most young women. In my town, or at least in my experience, men thought that women were weak. I hated being thought of as a lesser being.

I pulled myself away from that train of thought. I would deal with Amahté later. Right now, I wanted to eat something. But first, I had to dress.

I opened the dresser drawers, rifling through the contents. I had been right—the contents were much less formal than those of the wardrobe. Instead of choosing a dress, I chose a simple, long-sleeved tunic, with a longer skirt underneath. I felt so strange wearing long sleeves—my arms felt almost restricted. I wasn't used to wearing such heavy clothing.

I crossed the room. Opening the door revealed that no one was in sight, but that was just fine with me. I had always been better off taking care of myself. I left the room, closing the door softly behind me.

The hallway looked like it was made from limestone. Of course, that would be ridiculous, so it was most likely a limestone coating that gave the walls their white, shining color. Every door that I saw was closed. I tried to open them, but they were locked, too. Finally, I came to an open door.

This time, luck was with me; I had found the kitchens. I walked in cautiously, not sure if I was allowed to be here. I found an open container; it turned out to be the breadbox. I helped myself to a few slices, then went to look for some cheese to go with it.

I was lucky again; I found cheese *and* beef. Usually I couldn't afford beef; it was just too expensive for a farmhand. I usually got stuck with fish. I helped myself to the beef, then washed it down with a glass of fine wine. It tasted like it had come straight from the palace.

"Oh!"

I jumped, spilling the wine. I hadn't heard anyone enter the room. I turned. It was a servant; she had probably been assigned to the kitchen and had taken a break. She looked panicked to find me here.

"W-Who are you?" she stammered. This new girl was short, but she was definitely a little chubby. The slight roundness in her cheeks gave her a childish look, as did the curly brown ponytail.

"I'm Fala," I answered. What could be the harm in telling her who I was? "Who are you?"

She frowned. "Fala...oh! You are the guest of Master Amahté and Master Akori!" She paused for a quick curtsy. "Pleased to meet you, ma'am. My name is Amisi." I nodded, uncomfortable with the formalities.

Amisi continued. "I should have recognized you. You see, I was the one who stocked your wardrobe, and I was there when Master Amahté brought you in to bed. Speaking of wardrobes, would you prefer to change into something lighter? It is rather warm out today."

"Oh, no," I replied. Warm? This was warm? Dear Ra, I was going to freeze to death! "I am used to much hotter temperatures...I had to work in them, so this is kind of cold for me."

Her eyes widened. "Really? You were a laborer?" I nodded. "Oh, that is...surprising. It is just that, when Master Akori said that we would be having a guest, I thought that he and Master Amahté were bringing someone of a higher class." She paused, seeming horrified by what she had just said, before blurting, "Not that you are not a good person, I am certain that you are, it is just that—"

"Amisi," I interrupted, "it's okay. I am not of a higher class, and I accept that. Actually, I would prefer that you *not* treat me as someone of a high class. It's awkward." Amisi sighed in relief. She went to the far corner of the kitchen, and returned with two wet cloths. I took one from her, despite her protests (she insisted that the second cloth was for after the first grew too dirty to use). While we were cleaning up the wine, Amisi attempted to start a new, less awkward conversation.

"So, how do you get along with Master Amahté?"

"Amisi, if you don't mind, could you just call him 'Amahté'? It's just too strange to think of him as 'Master.' And we get along pretty well. I get along better with Akori though, because he's the only one with any manners."

"Oh, my. Miss Fala—"

"Just Fala, alright?"

"Fala, then. I know it is not my place, but could you please not mention that to Master Khenti and Missus Miu?"

"His manners? And would those be his parents?" The twins barely mentioned their parents. Maybe this would be a good time to learn a little bit about them.

Amisi nodded. "Yes, they are. I do mean not to complain about his manners. Akori, even though his manners are splendid, is not the focus of his parents. They pay far more attention to Amahté, and, as a result, he has little freedom. He tries to be himself, and he rebels often. But that just makes them pay even more attention to him."

"Why are they so concerned about Amahté and not Akori?"

"Because Amahté is the one who shall inherit his Ab's estate. Master Khenti chose Amahté because, even though Akori is older, Amahté looks more like his parents. They do not really know where Akori inherited his looks from."

"Why don't Amahté's parents just give inheritance rights to Akori?" I suggested. "That way, everyone would be satisfied." Amisi shook her head at my suggestion.

"I think that Akori would do very well...he is kind and patient, and he is fair. Not everyone would be satisfied, though. Master Khenti wants Amahté to take his place because Amahté looks more like him than Akori. Between you and me, miss, Master Khenti was always a bit self-centered." I laughed, and she grinned. But then her face grew serious.

"Quite a few years ago, something happened between the twins and their Ab. I do not remember it very well, as I am only a few years older than the twins, but my Mwt told me about it." I started—she was older than the twins? I never would have guessed! "When Amahté and Akori were five or six years old, Khenti tried to get rid of Akori. He planned on selling him into slavery in the human world. It would have worked, too, because Akori did not yet have his wings or tail, and the human world would have smothered his body. He would have died.

"The worst part was that everyone agreed with Master Khenti's decision...here, in this realm, it is believed that one twin will always be good and one will always be evil. That is how it was with the High Gods Osiris and Set, and no one wants a repeat of that. No one challenged Master Khenti except for Amahté. If it were not for him, Akori would not be here right now. I do not know exactly what he did, but it was enough to force Master Khenti to keep Akori. That is why they are so close now. The twins, I mean." I stared at her. What kind of person would try to sell their own child? It was no wonder that Akori was so loyal to Amahté!

Amisi saw my discomfort. "I am sorry, Fala. I should not have told you that."

"No, no, it's alright!" I said. But I said it too quickly.

She grinned again. "I wish I could stay and talk with you more. I cannot, though; I must finish my chores." I nodded, and we said our good-byes. Then I was alone. I put away the wine (or what was left of it), and headed for the door. Amisi had closed it behind her, so I opened the door—

And walked right into Amahté.

He blinked. "Fala? What are you doing here?"

"Well, like I said, humans need nourishment. And I am, in fact, a human." He still seemed surprised. I sighed. "Are you going to stand there all day, Amahté, or are you going to let me leave?"

"Oh," he said. He seemed to realize that he was standing in the doorway. He stepped back, letting me through. I started to walk back to the room I was using, and he followed.

"I was looking for you," he stated. "You had Akori and me worried," he paused, as if considering what he had just said. Then he changed the subject. "Our Mwt wants to see you about the amulet." I stopped, and turned to face him.

"What about it? I already told you everything I know. Why does she need to see me?"

"She doesn't believe me. She wants to speak with you

in person."

"Doesn't she believe Akori? Or hasn't she asked him?"

Amahté hesitated. "She…doesn't consider Akori's messages worth hearing. Our Ab is like that, too. They only wanted one child…and they were disappointed when they had twins. In our family, it's considered ideal for each generation to consist of two parents and one child. More often than not, if a second child is born, the parents try to…get rid of it. That is considered the right thing to do."

I stared at him, sure that I couldn't be hearing him correctly. In Egypt, it was true that more often than not one of the twins would die, but to get rid of a perfectly healthy child? Amisi had told me the same thing, but to hear it again from someone who had to live with it on a daily basis…

"What do you think?" I said softly, when I realized that he had been serious.

He fidgeted for a moment, then answered, "I don't agree with my parents' views. They are trying to convince me, but so far it hasn't worked. They probably won't give up anytime soon, though."

"Convince you? How are they trying to do that?"

"Bribery. They keep sending for goddesses and demigoddesses, hoping that one of them will catch my interest. I turn them all down; they're so shallow. It gets annoying." He grinned at that. He was obviously proud of himself. I grinned back. "But my parents keep trying. They think that they're being subtle."

"Maybe that's where Akori gets it from," I joked. "You know, you really should try to teach him subtlety. He is...not very good at it, to say the least."

"I know," he replied. "I have tried to teach him. He has some kind of mental block. This morning, he kept telling me that you and I would 'make each other happy.' He said it at least ten times, and—" He stopped, realizing what he had just said. He blushed, and stammered out, "Um...c-come on, we have to go see Mwt," before practically running away. I stood there for a moment, unsure of what I should do, then swore and ran after him.

"Amahté, wait! Wait a minute!" He turned without really taking the time to stop. As a result, he tripped over his own tail. I was still moving, and we crashed into each other with enough force to knock us both to the ground. And Amahté landed directly on top of me.

We both looked at each other, stunned into silence. Then we burst out laughing.

"Wow, very impressive." I laughed. "You managed to take us both out in one try!"

"Me?" he choked out. "You were the one who told me to stop! I was just listening to you!"

I laughed harder. "I didn't think that you would actually listen to me! You never have before!" We were laughing so hard that we could barely breathe. When we finally stopped, we had to catch our breath. Amahté caught his first. He stood up, then offered me his hand. I took it and he pulled me up. We looked at each other, then burst out laughing again. Anyone who was watching us would have thought that we had some serious issues...and they probably would have been right.

"So," Amahté said, "am I listening to you now?"

I shrugged. "I don't know. It's your choice, not mine. But I think that you would be better off listening to me when I tell you to do something."

"Oh? And why is that?"

"Because...if you don't...I will never make you tea again!"

"Then I better not listen. I hated your tea." We both laughed again. He was such a dork; but I guess that I was, too. Oh, well. There wasn't much that I could do about that.

"Fala?"

"Yes?"

"On a more serious note, my Mwt really would like to see you. If we could just..." I nodded, and he led me away.

"Fala?" Amahté asked again. "I have tonight off from my training with Ab. Usually, I spend the night either alone or with Akori, but...would you like to have supper with me?"

"Sure," I answered. "But no tea." He laughed, and we continued to talk. Fortunately for both of us, we didn't fall down again.

Amahté led me through the twisting hallways that made up his house. I was glad that he was with me; I would have gotten lost if I had tried to go by myself. I didn't have the greatest sense of direction in the world.

Amahté's Mwt was waiting in a room at the end of a

dead-end hallway. I wasn't really sure what to expect from a goddess, so I was grateful when she spoke first.

"So, Amahté, this is the human?" She looked at me apologetically. "I'm sorry—that was rather blunt, wasn't it?"

"It's fine," I assured her. "I don't mind. You have to do what you have to do." She looked relieved that she hadn't offended me. I didn't see what the big deal was; I was perfectly happy as a human.

The twins' Mwt looked very much like Akori, but with Amahté's skin tone. She had long hair, so long that even braided it fell almost to her knees, and it was the same color as Akori's. What did Amisi mean, no one knew where Akori got his looks from? They looked so similar. I cringed, realizing that the denial probably had something to do with the fact that Akori was the 'unwanted' twin.

Her wings and tail were a light, almost fragile-colored lavender, and her wings were slightly darker than her tail. She wasn't what I had been expecting at all!

"I am sorry," she said again, "but I have forgotten your name."

"My name is Fala," I told her. Was she this polite all the time?

"What a beautiful name!" she exclaimed. "You may call me Miu."

I nodded, not quite sure how I should respond. Amahté seemed uncomfortable, too.

"Oh," Miu said, "you must be hungry."

"No, actually, I just ate—"

"Nonsense!" She clapped her hands, and the door opened.

"Amisi!" I cried. She looked up in surprise, and her expression changed to joy.

"Fala!"

"*Miss* Fala," Miu corrected.

"No, no," I said hastily, "just Fala is fine. I prefer to not use titles, since I don't have one in Egypt." Miu looked surprised for a moment, then composed herself and nodded for Amisi to leave. She obeyed, looking confused as to why she had been called, only to be sent away moments later.

Miu looked after her for a moment, then said, "That was rather rude of me. I should not send the servants away directly after calling them in. I will apologize later." She turned back to me. "Unfortunately, we have more important things to worry about. I think it would be best for us to discuss the Osiris Amulet now, yes?"

I nodded. She was so polite; I made a mental note to have Akori teach me etiquette later. "What would you like to know?"

"Whatever you are able to tell me."

"Amahté said…I thought that you could do something to look at—what is it called? The trace on the amulet?"

Miu frowned, and I could tell that I had struck a nerve. "We *should* be able to. However, there is some sort of power preventing us from doing this; we can barely get a fix on its aura. It is almost as if the amulet does not want its owner to be found. Although, that may be what it was designed to do."

"What do you mean?"

"Lord Osiris has many enemies, including his brother. If it were so simple as to follow the aura of the necklace, or to read the trace upon it, then it would not be a very useful protection. As it is, we will simply need to do things the old-fashioned way. Now, Amahté said that it belonged to your Mwt?"

"Yes. Well, as far as I know. My Mwt always insisted that it was a wedding gift from my Ab. I never had the chance to ask him myself; he left my Mwt just before I was born."

"Do you know his name?" she inquired.

"No," I answered. I suddenly realized that I knew almost as little as they did. "My Mwt never said his name. She started to say it once, when she thought I was in another room, but then she saw me. I don't even know if he is still alive."

She considered this for a moment, then smiled, despite the fact that I had been no help at all. "Alright then, Fala. You may go. I merely wished to see if you knew his name. Thank you."

I nodded, and I left the room with Amahté. When we were out in the hall, Amahté said, "Now you see why Akori has such excessive manners. He's too much like our Mwt."

I laughed at that. How could I not, when it was so true? Still, I scolded him for it. "You really shouldn't make fun of your brother, you know. He is very loyal to you."

"I know," he answered quietly. "He shouldn't be. He

should get away from here, regardless of whether or not I can go with him."

"Why?" I asked. "Why does he have to leave?"

"He doesn't *have* to, I guess. I just think that he should. Ab really doesn't like him, and Mut ignores him most of the time. I think that he should go somewhere where his talents are appreciated."

We walked in silence for a few moments. Then Amahté said, "Usually, Akori can tell when two people would make each other happy. That…is one of his talents." He said no more, but I knew what he was hinting at. I didn't answer. I refused to rush into this blindly like some star-crossed lover, as I had seen many boys in my village do. Those boys usually ended up as beggars. So I chose to change the subject.

"Hey, Amahté? When do people eat lunch here?" In Egypt, or at least in my town, I would never ask that question. Most of the people in my town only ate two meals a day: breakfast and dinner. If you could even afford enough food for a third meal, your work usually gave you no time for it. So, most of us stayed satisfied with a two-meal diet.

"Lunch? Isn't that what you were eating in the kitchen?"

"No. I was having breakfast."

"Fala, you slept through breakfast. Ra is already at his highest in the sky." Well, I suppose that would explain why I had been so hungry; I had missed a meal!

"Oh…well, what should I do now? I have quite a bit of time left before our dinner."

He shrugged. "How am I supposed to know? Maybe you could…do your makeup?"

"Makeup?" I laughed. "I never wear makeup. That's for the wealthy, for their galas and parties. And I wouldn't wear it even if I *could* afford it; it's a waste of time. What made you say that?" He had been around me long enough to see that I didn't do that sort of thing.

"I don't know. I thought that that was what most human women did in their spare time."

"And the fact that you've never seen me do that before…?"

"I don't know. Maybe you didn't have enough time, or enough to barter with? I just…I don't know. It was the only thing I could think of."

I laughed again. "You need to get out more, Amahté."

~*~

I ended up cleaning the room I was using, and Amahté ended up helping me. We had nothing better to do, and we needed to use up quite a bit of time. In the end, we used a lot of time as well as energy, so when it was time for dinner, we were both starving. Amahté insisted that the location of our dinner should be a surprise, so he led me there after blindfolding me.

"Are we almost there?" I asked. I was getting sick of being kept, quite literally, in the dark. I got my answer when Amahté pulled off the blindfold.

"Ta-da! My personal hide-away!" he exclaimed.

It was beautiful. We were up on a terrace, with a wonderful view of the grounds around us. I could see a colorful garden disappearing around the corner of the estate, and beyond the carefully kept lands there was a sprawling forest.

Someone had already been here to set up for us. Next to the railing, there was a small table, full of delicious (and expensive)-looking food.

I walked over to one of the chairs, unsure of what to do. Amahté was there before me, pulling out the chair so I could sit down. I did, and he took the seat next to mine. For a few moments, we sat in silence. Then Amahté offered me a drink, and we began to talk.

"So," I began, "your Mwt seems…nice."

Amahté laughed. "Actually, this is her on a bad day. She's always been overly polite. She balances out my Ab."

"Is your Ab…outgoing?" I asked.

"Outgoing?" He laughed again. It was a harsh, regretful sound this time, not like those I had heard from him before. "I suppose you could say it that way, if you were trying to be kind."

We lapsed into silence. After a few minutes, we moved onto more open subjects. We continued to talk, even after we had finished our meal.

Finally, when it grew dark, Amahté said, "I really had a good time, Fala. Perhaps we could do this again tomorrow?"

"Of course," I answered. We stood to leave. I took one

last look at the beautiful scene before me; then I followed Amahté out the door.

And so went my days. In the mornings, I would sleep in, then get up and eat a late breakfast by myself. Afterwards, I would insist on cleaning up after myself, and then I would find chores to fill my morning. This behavior continuously baffled Amahté and Akori, who usually ended up helping me. I would have lunch with Akori in my room, and then the twins and I would fill the afternoon with games and conversation. Usually, these conversations ended in at least one of us laughing uncontrollably.

A few times, they took me to their library. That was one of my favorite places to go, because I loved to read; my Mwt had taught me. Many of my memories of her were of the two of us, curled up together, reading a story. Of course, we could only afford four different scrolls. I still read sometimes; my ex-boarder had kept a few in the room he had been using. When he left on business, I would brave the stench and read what he had to offer.

Then, in the evening, Amahté would take me to his balcony for dinner. This was one of my favorite parts of the day. Of course, Akori was wonderful, but I had almost nothing in common with him. We tried to understand each other, but when I was with Amahté, things just fell into place. We could talk for hours without any awkward silences.

After a while I got used to the cooler temperatures. The long sleeves and skirts slowly retreated into what I was more used to wearing. The twins teased that I should just stay there with them—going back to Egypt might overheat my "poor little human body".

Sometimes, Miu would call me to her room to try to pick my brain. It didn't do much good; I had already told her everything that I knew, but she didn't seem ready to accept that. She even tried hypnosis once or twice, which only resulted in my own embarrassment.

Everything was nice, and the scenery was beautiful, but it just wasn't home. As poor as I was in Egypt, I knew how everything worked: the foods, the markets, the social standings. Here I just felt out of place. And things seemed kind of boring...at least for a while.

One particular night, just after we had finished our meal, Amahté pushed his plate away and stood. This was unusual for him. We usually talked for at least an hour before we even began to consider leaving.

I had been here for almost a full moon cycle now, and I had never seen him look this awkward.

He cleared his throat. "Fala, I have been thinking about...well, about what Akori said. And I was wondering if...you would allow me to court you? If it's alright with you, I'd like to give it a try."

I stared at him for a moment. He obviously didn't know what he was doing when it came to romance. Poor guy. "Well, I guess that would be fine." It couldn't hurt, could it?

His face lit up, and I could see that I had made him happy. I tried not to think about the fact that, eventually, I was going to go back to Egypt. We would have to figure that out…but I felt confident that we could make something work. Even if this relationship didn't work out, we could still be friends…right?

That night, when we left the balcony, we left holding hands. And I didn't mind one bit.

~*~

After Amahté and I left the balcony, we went to see Akori. He had been unable to hide his excitement when we had announced that we were courting. Actually, Amahté had announced it. For once in my life, I felt too shy to speak. Now the three of us were lying on Akori's balcony. Well, it wasn't really a balcony; it was more of a ledge. But it was big enough for all three of us to lie comfortably, while looking up at the night sky.

The twins had shown me a bunch of different constellations; I hadn't known that there were so many! When their knowledge of the stars finally ended, we started coming up with our own.

"Look, Fala," Amahté said, "that cluster there could be you!"

"I see it!" exclaimed Akori. He was still quieter than Amahté, though not as quiet as I had once thought. Still, it was nice to be able to see him relax and be comfortable with himself. It was even rarer here than it had been in my home— it made me sad to see him constantly tense, constantly watching over his shoulder and fighting for approval that he knew he wouldn't get.

"If that's me," I countered, "then those two on either side of 'me' are you two." Amahté pouted, but soon brightened. It was impossible for him to be quiet for long.

After some time, Amahté sighed. "Gods, the sky is so clear tonight. It's beautiful."

That confused me. "…Do gods always swear by themselves?" I asked.

"What are you talking about?"

"Aren't you two gods?" They both burst out laughing—definitely not the response that I had been hoping for. "Hello? What's so funny?!"

"I am sorry," said Akori, trying to catch his breath. "We probably should have told you. We are not full gods; we are only demigods, like the rest of our family. It is a bit like being priests in the pharaoh's palace."

"Did you think that we were gods this whole time?" Amahté was still laughing. I punched him in the arm—that shut him up. Well, mostly; every few moments I would hear him chuckle quietly to himself.

We went on like that for the rest of the night, until I finally dozed off in the early hours of dawn.

~*~

When I first woke up, I fought against the real world. My dreams had been amazing, and I struggled to hold onto them. I failed, however, and was brought back into reality.

My first brilliant thought of the day was, 'Gods, I'm so stiff.'
Isn't that poetic? For a moment, I couldn't figure out why I
was so uncomfortable, but then I realized that the twins and I
had fallen asleep on the stone balcony. I guess that that
would explain it. Beside me, Akori yawned and sat up.
Blinking the sleep from his eyes, he looked over at the still
sleeping Amahté and laughed. I shushed him, but he just
laughed harder.

 "Do not worry," he explained. "Amahté is the heaviest
sleeper I know. An entire army could race past, and he could
still sleep through it! But if you want him to wake up…" He
trailed off, grinning evilly.

 Before I could stop him, he ran over to Amahté, rolled
him onto his back, and elbowed him in the stomach. Amahté's
eyes shot open, and he threw Akori over his shoulder and
into the wall! And then they both got up laughing!

 "Well," I commented, "that was an interesting way to
start the morning." That just made them laugh harder. After
they had calmed down enough to breathe, we stood, and
went to breakfast. Actually, we started to go to breakfast.
Before we were halfway across the room, another girl ran in. I
saw that she was human, like me, but unlike me, she was
panicked and breathless.

 "Master Amahté," she began, "I am terribly sorry to
bother you, but your Ab has just sent a message. He's
coming back tonight, and he is—" she broke off, staring at
me with wide eyes. I stared back, trying to figure out what
was so strange to her. I had never been much of a morning

person, but I couldn't look *that* bad.

"He's what?" Amahté prompted. "What is it?"

"O-Oh," she stuttered, "he is bringing some of the higher-ups with him, and he is having a gala in their honor, so he would like everything to look its best." With that, she bowed, threw another strange glance at me, and left the room.

"Humans," I heard Amahté mutter.

"And what is wrong with humans?" I countered.

Amahté blushed, something he rarely did. "Well…I meant servants. Yeah, that's what I meant."

"Explain," I demanded. I wasn't buying that lame excuse for a minute.

"Well…here, humans are seen as inferior. That's why she looked so surprised when she saw you; she's not used to seeing humans and demigods as equals."

"She should get used to seeing it. I'm not going to let you two treat them poorly just because they are humans!" They both nodded. "Wait, Akori, why are you nodding? You didn't say anything."

"I just…felt like I should nod…"

"I don't mean to offend you, Fala," Amahté interjected. "That's just the way I was raised to think. I don't mean to do it. Most of the time I don't even notice."

"Well, that's going to stop now. Alright?" Amahté nodded again. I wasn't exactly sure what I could do to punish him, but he didn't need to know that.

"So," Akori said, changing the subject. He needed

some serious lessons; he still didn't know how to be subtle. "It seems that Ab is coming home early, so you'll be able to meet him. However, there is a catch."

"Catch? What catch?"

"You don't mind wearing gowns and makeup, do you?"

"Gowns? And *makeup*?" I was horrified. I never wore gowns and makeup—ever. I didn't even do anything fancy with my hair. I just pulled it back into a ponytail. I was probably the only girl in all of Egypt who didn't just shave her head…

Amahté saw my face and said, "It doesn't have to be too fancy. Just enough to be a gown. And don't worry. I can have someone pick out a dress for you, and then they can do your hair."

"Do I get to do anything around here?" I asked. "Or do I just sit around like a lump?" Amahté and Akori just laughed.

Chapter Four

"I feel absolutely ridiculous!" I said again. No one seemed to hear my protests…again. Amisi had picked out a floor-length gown with long, full sleeves, and a neckline that ran across my collarbone. My dress was a light powder blue; it matched Amahté's wings. Which was one of the reasons that I felt ridiculous. What made it even worse was the fact that Amisi was doing my hair, too.

"Oh, don't complain, Fala," Amahté said for the thousandth time. That was easy for him to say. He was already finished getting ready. I had had to sit through Amisi putting my makeup on, which it seemed that she didn't get to do very often. She had used this fact to guilt me into sitting still for her for over an hour. I didn't understand why I couldn't just wear a wig—that's what all the noblewomen did back home.

Amahté and Akori got off easy. They both wore simple tunics with simple leggings underneath. Amahté's tunic was slightly darker than his wings, and Akori's were slightly lighter. All three of us wore simple bracelets, and I, of course, wore the amulet. Amisi had tried to talk me into wearing a heavy gold neck piece with matching arm bands, but that was where I put my foot down. I would not look ridiculous *and* leave my Mwt's amulet behind.

After Amisi had finished fixing my hair, she turned to the twins. "Does she look acceptable, Master Akori?"

"Hmm?" Akori turned, blushing. I snickered—he'd probably just been caught daydreaming. "Oh, yes, she looks wonderful, Amisi. Thank you very much."

Amisi curtsied, blushing at the compliment. Then I got a lecture on keeping my hair up. Which I tuned out. When she finally finished, Akori gave me what was supposed to be a pep talk.

"Be sure to make eye contact," he said, "but try not to be challenging. I know that that is against your nature, but please try. But do not pretend to be nervous, either. And—"

"Akori!" I interrupted. "Calm down. I'll do my best. I'm sure I can manage; I'm not going into battle." He nodded. And then all three of us were off to greet the demigods' Ab, something that I was *not* looking forward to. I hadn't heard a single positive thing about him. But I didn't really have much of a choice, and I generally tried not to judge people that I didn't know. So I was trying to be on my 'best behavior' (as Amahté had put it) for this gala, and for the meeting before it.

The twins' Ab was waiting for us in the room where I had first met Miu. As we headed down the hallway, I whispered, "Akori, what's your Ab's name? I forgot."

"It is Khenti," he told me. "But…you probably would be better off if you did not address him by name; he is very old-fashioned." I nodded; I could remember to do that, at least. I tried to forget what I had heard about Khenti, so that I could meet him without making any unfair judgments.

That plan failed miserably, but not because of me. As soon as we entered the room, Khenti said, "Wakhashem, you will leave now. This is important; I don't want you to screw it up. Now go." Akori nodded miserably and left. I started to go after him, to bring him back, but I realized that that probably wasn't the greatest idea. I didn't want Akori to have to stand here and be treated like that—Khenti had no right to call him a little fool!

After Akori had gone, Khenti looked me over. Whatever he saw, he didn't seem to like it; his frown only grew more pronounced. I certainly didn't like the looks of him, either. He had cropped black hair and a nose like a hawk's beak. The lines in his face made it seem like he was always frowning, but it was his eyes that bothered me the most. Those were the eyes of someone cruel, of someone who was willing to crush anyone and anything that got in their way.

I wasn't sure if he was waiting for me to speak, or if he was just looking. I wanted to tell him to stop looking and actually say something. I wasn't an exhibit. Hadn't he ever heard of common courtesy?

Amahté cleared his throat, breaking the silence. "Ab, this is Fala…the one I told you about? She's my…girlfriend." It was still sort of awkward, hearing him say that out loud.

But it was easier to deal with than the silence, and it was better than just standing around in a glaring contest. Oh, wait—I wasn't supposed to be glaring back. Oops. I almost regretted it, but then Khenti decided to open his mouth again.

"Amahté, what are you *thinking?*" he sneered. "She is a *human*. How is it that you turn down every goddess you meet, only to accept this...this...*filth*. It isn't right to marry beneath you."

I gritted my teeth, trying to stay silent. I kept saying to myself, *'This is for the twins, this is for the twins...'*

Amahté spoke for me. "Fala is *not* filth. She is an intelligent, kind young woman, and she is far better than any of those shallow goddesses. Akori thinks that she's great, too. He—"

"I don't give a damn about what that half-wit *nothing* thinks. He's not worth my time. And—"

"*You* are the one not worthy of *his* time!" I hissed, losing my temper. "Akori is an amazing person, and you are nothing but an arrogant—"

"*And,*" Khenti yelled over me, "just because she has the Osiris amulet doesn't mean that you should—"

"Oh," I said, "so you want him to be a shallow monster like you? Ra *forbid* that he actually takes a person for who they are—"

"Listen, you worthless child of a whore—"

He was cut off, thankfully, by a knock on the door. Without waiting for an invitation, the door opened, and Miu entered the room. I was glad; she, at least, didn't constantly bad-mouth people.

"Khenti, dear," she murmured, "you are not giving Fala a hard time, are you? She really is a wonderful girl, very determined and independent. You should give her a chance." Again, she didn't pause to wait for an answer, and turned to me. "Is eleven too late for you? Amahté told me that humans need more sleep than we do. And we do have to meet again later on." I knew that she was trying to be polite, but I couldn't help feeling embarrassed. Being around the brothers' family made me feel like a child: fragile and helpless. As ridiculous as it was, I felt that I had to defend myself.

"That is fine," I said tersely. "I stay up later than most humans anyway."

She nodded, and took Khenti's arm. "Come on, my dear, we mustn't be late. It would be rude." And with that, the couple left the room. Akori entered moments later.

"Akori, why did you leave?" I demanded. "He had no right to—"

"Yes, he did," he told me gently. "Fala, I don't think you understand just how powerful he is here. He *owns* this place…and he controls who can live here and who can't. If I disobeyed him, he could throw me out, and I wouldn't have anywhere to go. Plus, he's my Ab; I have to listen to him."

When he put it that way, I knew that he really didn't have a choice. In Egypt, a disobedient child could be beaten, sold into slavery…all kinds of horrible things. And no one ever helped the children, or the entire village would ostracize them.

I frowned. "Alright…but that doesn't mean that I have to like it. Or him." I turned to Amahté. "I was not joking, your Ab is a bastard." They both laughed at that, but the sound was almost painful.

"Stop stalling, Fala," Akori teased. "We have to go to the gala now." I groaned. "Don't worry; it's not that big of a deal. It'll be over before you know it. Now come on." Akori took one of my hands; Amahté took the other. Then we left to go to a (hopefully) uneventful evening.

The entrance to the ballroom was just down the hall. A huge, elegant staircase led the way into the actual room, which was beautifully decorated with all kinds of ornaments. Unfortunately, no one seemed to be paying much attention to the decorations. They were all focused on me.

"I guess they've been expecting you," Amahté whispered. "Oh, well. People will talk." Normally, I would have elbowed him in the ribs. But at the moment I was just trying to concentrate on not falling down.

When we got to the bottom, I almost wished that I *had* fallen down. Then, maybe, I would have hit my head and gotten knocked out. That would have been bliss compared to the Ra-damned gala. Pretty much every god, goddess, and demigod wanted to talk to me, which would have been nice if they weren't treating me like a child. They all spoke to me like they weren't sure if I could understand them or not; it was insulting. Sure, I wasn't the most educated human there was, but I knew enough to know what was going on.

Take the demigod Baki, for example. He actually asked Amahté if I knew how to do anything other than manual labor! I told him that I could speak for myself, and that I could do far more than just 'manual labor.' And he wasn't even ashamed! He actually seemed surprised, then turned back to Amahté and said that 'for a *human*, she seems fairly capable.' And I had always thought that my species was rude.

Seeing as Amahté was to inherit his Ab's estate, though, we couldn't exactly leave. Although it was probably just as bad for Akori as it was for me. If he wasn't being ignored, he was being pushed around. And not in the figurative sense, either; people would run into him, full speed, and then spit at him for it. He didn't even defend himself. He would just apologize and walk away.

"Why do you do that?" I asked after a particularly nasty goddess had walked away. "Why do you just stand there and let them push you around?"

Akori just shrugged. "I'm worthless in their eyes because I'm not inheriting my Ab's estate. But I can't do anything about it because that also means that I have no power in my family. Only Amahté does, and our Ab can overrule him." I didn't question him anymore after that. I was afraid to hear the answers he could give.

The gala seemed to last for an impossibly long time, but it was finally over. I nearly collapsed with relief; I didn't think that I could've taken one more god questioning me. Of course, Amahté had had almost no trouble at all.

"That wasn't so bad, was it, Fala?" he laughed. That was easy for *him* to say. He hadn't had everyone looking him over like an animal. And he hadn't had to worry about this damn hairstyle. I would have to make sure that Amisi kept it simple if there was a next time. Akori grimaced; he knew how I felt, because he had been worse off than me.

But I couldn't exactly worry about any of that now. Now, the three of us had to go and finish our little 'meeting' with Khenti. I wondered if he would be just as bad as he had been earlier, or if he had just made a bad first impression. Either way, if he got snippy now, I would snap right back at him. The gala had lasted longer than expected, and I was exhausted. Amahté had told me that we could postpone the meeting, but there was no way that I would give Khenti a reason to gloat.

Oblivious to my inner ranting, Amahté continued to talk. "Fala, I know that our Ab wasn't exactly kind to you earlier—"

I snorted. He hadn't been anywhere *near* kind; he had been downright rude.

Amahté ignored me and went on. "—and you have every right to defend yourself if you have to. But I would really prefer if you would just try to be patient... and humor him. Mwt will be there, so things shouldn't get too bad." I rolled my eyes, but I hoped that he was right. I just wanted to get this whole mess sorted out.

By this time, we were right outside the room that

Khenti was in. It was the same room as before, but as we stepped inside, I saw that it was much darker. I wondered idly if Khenti had done this to try and scare me, or if it was just because it was later.

Miu was there this time. I was glad for that; maybe Khenti would act differently around his wife.

"Wakhashem," Khenti sneered, "I thought I told you to leave. I can't figure out if you're disobedient or just plain stupid." Okay, maybe he wouldn't be any different than the first time. Akori bowed, and began to leave, but I grabbed his arm.

"If you want to talk to me, then Akori stays. He deserves to be included just as much as Amahté does. And he is *not* a fool." Khenti fumed, but nodded. I could care less; I had tried twice to give him the benefit of the doubt, and he had blown it both times.

Akori stood slightly behind me, next to Amahté. Throughout all of this, Miu didn't say a single word; in fact, she seemed more emotionless than I had ever seen her. How could she stand there and watch her son be treated like that? Why didn't Amahté say anything?

For a few awkward moments, we stood in silence. Then Khenti spoke. "The Osiris amulet. Where did you get it from?" I paused, taken aback. Hadn't I already told this story to both the twins and Miu? I glanced over my shoulder, but the brothers seemed just as confused as I was.

Akori spoke up in my defense. "Ab, she already told Mwt where she got it. She—"

"Be quiet, you filthy mongrel!" Khenti snapped. Akori let out a quiet whimper. "If I *want* to hear your worthless opinion, I'll ask for it. I was asking the human girl. Now," he said, turning back to me, "where did you get it?"

"From my Mwt," I told him. "Do you want me to tell the whole story again? I wasn't aware that demi-gods could be *deaf*." I couldn't help feeling a little bit annoyed. How many times did I have to say something before it got through to them?

"Don't give me that lousy cover-up. I want to know what *really* happened."

"That doesn't mean anything," I told him. "That is what really happened. My Mwt got it from my Ab as a wedding gift, and she gave it to me."

"Ha! Do you really think that I am going to fall for that story? We all know you stole it. How else would you come by something that valuable? Don't pretend to be innocent!" Amahté and Akori looked horrified. Oh Ra…I knew that they would believe me, but would they say that here? Or would they be pressured into going against me?

Evidently, they were willing to take my side. Amahté shouted, "That's not true!" at the same time that Akori yelled, "She wouldn't do that!"

"Stop defending the human!" Khenti shouted at Akori, as if he had been the only one to speak. "She's even worse than *you*!"

That did it. "Don't talk to him like that!" I commanded. "He's your son!" Khenti, apparently, didn't like being told what to do. Before anyone could stop him, before anyone had time to react, he stepped forward and slapped me across the face. Amahté cried out, but Khenti ignored him and grabbed my necklace. In the split second that he held it, I realized that he wanted to yank it off my neck.

Even as I held that thought, my vision blurred around the edges, and I felt a sharp pain in my head. Khenti pulled his hand back and hissed in pain. And then I collapsed.

~*~

My head…my head hurt so badly; it felt like it was about to explode. The shaking didn't help. Wait…shaking? Why was I shaking?

I forced my eyes open and saw Amahté, two inches from my face, holding me by the shoulders and shaking me like my life depended on it.

"Fala?" he said. He sounded panicked. I wondered vaguely how long I had been out, or where I was. Akori looked worried, too…but that was probably an understatement. If he didn't stop biting his nails soon, he was going to end up chewing his hand off. I noticed, for the first time, that Amahté was trying to talk to me.

"Fala?" I heard Amahté say. I tried to sit up, then fell back again. I was too dizzy to move anywhere on my own…this was not how I had hoped the day would turn out…

"—own?" Amahté finished whatever he had been saying, but I hadn't caught any of it.

"What did you say?" I mumbled. Although, thanks to my spinning head (and the fact that I wasn't fully conscious), it sounded like garbled mush.

Amahté understood it, somehow. "I asked if you were okay, and if you thought you could walk on your own." Oh, thank goodness, he had finally stopped shaking me.

I rolled my eyes at him. "I don't...no...my head hurts...and I can't stand up if I don't want to fall down again. Where am I?" It still hurt if I tried to do anything but lie still, but I had to move sometime.

Amahté looked worried. "You don't know? We're still in my Ab's meeting room. Do you remember? We came here to talk to him about the amulet." I nodded. I could think a little clearer now, but not much. Just enough that I vaguely remembered where I was. I heard Amahté tell someone, "She doesn't know where she is. I think she's got a head wound." Oh, that was just what I needed right now. Well, that would explain why I couldn't stand up.

Akori came over and helped to get me into a sitting position, and my stomach lurched. I opened my mouth to tell them that I felt nauseous—

And threw up *all over.* Oh gods, that was disgusting. I gagged a few more times, but thankfully, I didn't puke again. Amahté held me close. I had to give him credit—if he was throwing up on me, I wasn't sure I would hold on to him.

I tried to sit up again, but the twins wouldn't let me this time. I let them stop me with a sigh; what would be the point in trying to stand? I would just fall and hit my head again.

Amahté let me calm my body down a bit, and then picked me up and carried me away.

The motion made my head spin. I was having trouble focusing; I couldn't exactly tell where I was. There were a few times when I realized that Amahté was speaking to me, and once my mind registered that he was putting me down on something soft. But I felt too woozy to really comprehend anything.

When my head finally stopped spinning, I was back in my room. Or, I guess, 'my' room, because it was only temporary. My memory was fuzzy, but I remembered going to meet Khenti. I remembered him going to take the amulet, and then pulling away in pain. And I vaguely recalled being on the ground while Amahté talked to me. But that was it.

Someone put a hand on my shoulder, making me jump. I squirmed out of their grip and backed away (almost falling off my bed in the process) before I realized that it was only Amahté.

"It's okay, Fala," he whispered. "You're back in your room. Everything's okay." He held out his arms, and I crawled into them. For a few moments, we sat like that; I liked him holding me. Plus, I needed the time to help sort out my thoughts. I tried to think back, to remember what had happened. But it was still so hazy…

As if he could read my thoughts, Amahté said, "You probably don't remember much, other than hitting your head. Right?" I nodded. "Well, to make a long story short, you fainted and hit your head, so now you have a mild concussion. You'll be alright, as long as you're careful for the next week or so."

"Gods, I can't believe I fainted...I swear, that has *never* happened before."

"Hmm, how do I know that you aren't lying to me?"

I punched him arm playfully. "Why would I lie? And really, there wasn't any reason for me to faint before...believe it or not, my life was normal before you and your brother showed up."

"Maybe you were just being too careful before."

"Does that mean I shouldn't be careful now?"

He made a face. "Please, *please* be careful. I really don't fancy getting thrown up on again."

I blushed, and he laughed. Then I recalled my most pressing question: "What happened back there? With your Ab, I mean." Was there no end to the strangeness that would find me?

"Well, I know *what* happened, I just don't know *why* it happened. Mwt doesn't really know either, but we're going to try to figure it out."

When he just stared at me, I said, "So...are you going to tell me what happened or...?"

"Oh, right...Ab tried to take the amulet from you, without your permission. One of the protective spells of the amulet...well, it knocked him out, actually. And he has a burn mark on his hand. But it shouldn't have happened."

Well I sure didn't see any problem with that. "Why not? He slapped me, he deserved it."

Amahté chuckled. "That's not what I meant. That particular spell shouldn't have been able to activate; it's only supposed to work for those who have a direct connection with Osiris." He was still holding me. I twisted around, so that we could see each other's faces.

"I told the truth," I insisted. "I don't know where my Ab got it, and if my Mwt didn't get it from him, then I don't know where she got it. But I didn't steal it. If you don't believe me, then—"

"Fala!" he interrupted. I stopped speaking. "I believe you. My Ab came up with that idea, through what we know about the amulet. There are thousands of different possibilities; my Ab only chose that one because he is prejudiced against humans."

I shook my head. "How can your family know practically *everything* about the amulet, right down to the spells it controls, and not know who it's supposed to belong to?"

He shrugged. "I don't know. The spells are one of the things that are documented; no one ever wrote down the name of Osiris's wife."

"Well, whoever was supposed to be writing this stuff down did a lousy job. And your Ab is doing a lousy job of interpreting it; there's no way that I could ever have a connection with Osiris. I would know about it." At least, I thought so. I racked my memory, trying to recall if my Mwt had ever said anything that could apply to this kind of situation.

But I gave that up pretty quickly—how in Ra's name could she have known anything about this?

"Like I said, that's my Ab's interpretation of the situation. That is why he was so convinced that you were lying to him earlier, and he's even surer of his theory now. My Mwt has been frantic, trying to show him that you're innocent. She thinks the amulet is just…well, 'confused' right now. It's treating you as the rightful heir because you inherited it legitimately."

I guessed that made sense…more sense than Khenti's theory, anyway. Wait, Miu! "Your Mwt is okay, right? She was standing right next to Khenti."

"She's fine. Actually, if the amulet hadn't hurt him, she probably would have. He definitely crossed the line; my Mwt would never let him get away with treating a guest like that." We both laughed at that, but Amahté laughed harder than I did. I was remembering something that I had thought earlier…

"Amahté? Why didn't you defend your brother?"

His smile faded, replaced by a wistful look. "Ah…I can't show how close we are. I've tried to defend him in the past; that only makes Ab treat him worse. I can't be with him all the time. Doing nothing defends him more than physically protecting him."

"…I understand."

"No," he sighed. "You don't. And I hope you never do."

I opened my mouth to respond, but just then I felt another sharp pain, this time in my chest, right where I wore the amulet. I reached up instinctively…and realized with horror that the amulet was gone. Instead, I wore a bruise that was already turning blue.

"Um…where did it go…?" Amahté whispered. I raised my gaze to meet his, and I could see his panic and confusion.

"If we lose the amulet…" I trailed off; I didn't need to finish. Khenti had gone crazy when I had had the amulet; there was no telling what he would do if I lost it.

Amahté and I both jumped up and began to search the room, even though we knew that we wouldn't find anything. We still had to try, in case it *was* there, for some strange reason. Of course, we didn't find it. After a full hour of searching, we gave up. It wasn't in my room.

I sat back on the bed. "Where else could it be?" I wondered. "How could it be anywhere but in this room?" I looked to Amahté, but he seemed just as clueless as I felt. I'd lost an important divine item, one that my Mwt had asked me to keep safe. Of course, she hadn't known its importance, but I still felt like I had failed her.

"I don't know what could have happened," Amahté said. "We shouldn't worry about it." I looked at him incredulously—really? He wanted me to not worry about it? "There's nothing we can do. It has to be here somewhere…we'll find it."

"I guess you're right," I sighed, and glanced down. With a start, I realized that I was still in the gown that I had worn to the gala. "Ugh. I'm still wearing this thing."

Amahté laughed at me. "What's the matter? You don't

like it? You'll hurt Amisi's feelings." I threw a pillow at him. He threw it right back; I caught it just before it hit my face. I thought that he would be done after that, but when I lowered the pillow in surrender, he tackled me. One minute, I was sitting upright, and the next, Amahté was pinning me to the bed, his face inches from mine.

And then there was no distance. I felt the warmth from his lips spread throughout my entire body, and for a few moments, nothing else mattered. Not finding the amulet, not dealing with Khenti. At that moment Amahté was the only thing that mattered in the world.

All too soon, he pulled his lips from mine. I was so stunned that I couldn't even begin to follow; I couldn't smack him for grinning at me like a lunatic. By the time I had recovered from the kiss, he had made it to the door.

"Where are you going?" I pouted. "Is that all I get?"

He laughed, ecstatic. "Well, on a more serious note, I really should tell my Mwt and Akori that the amulet is missing. And you should really get some sleep. Good night, Fala." And with that, he left.

When I saw that he wasn't coming back, I went to change my clothes; I couldn't exactly sleep in a gown. After some searching, I found a shorter night-dress that would work. Amisi had filled my wardrobe with warmer clothes when I told her I was cold all the time. I was fine now, but I would feel badly if she had to change it all again.

I changed into the night-dress, then went to inspect the bruise on my collarbone. I wasn't exactly sure where I had gotten it from, but I hadn't noticed it until the amulet vanished. Maybe it was a backlash of magic—if it could burn Khenti's hand, then why couldn't it bruise me?

I looked in the mirror…and froze, unable to understand what I was seeing. What I had thought to be a bruise was now a perfect likeness of the amulet that I had worn that afternoon; the only difference was that this was *embedded in my skin.*

"……AMAHTÉ!!!" I knew I shouldn't scream, but what was I supposed to do? There was a *divine item* in my skin! Was I supposed to stay *calm*?! Screaming brought on a sharp pain, the same kind of pain that I had felt when the amulet vanished. "Oh, gods, what now…?" I doubled over, clutching my collarbone, and generally praying that Amahté would be the one to find me.

Well, he did find me there first, but he wasn't alone. It seemed like his whole family was there: Akori, Miu, Khenti, his cousins, and a ridiculous amount of people that I just didn't know. Fortunately, Miu ushered out everyone except for Amahté and Akori.

"Fala? Fala, what's wrong?" Amahté kept saying. But I couldn't answer him; the pain had spread to my throat, and that made it nearly impossible to talk.

I managed to choke out a small "Ouch," and that was enough. The twins seemed to understand that I was hurting too much to talk right now, and Amahté pulled me close. I let him hold me, waiting for the pain to fade. As it did, I looked around, trying to make sense of what had just happened.

Everything was so…sharp, and focused. My vision had always been kind of blurry, but now I felt like I could see *everything*. And I could hear things, too: Khenti complaining to Miu, the relatives forming their own rumors and theories about what had happened. What was going on?

I took a deep breath; the pain was completely gone now. "Amahté…I think I found the amulet," I said shakily. The twins looked confused, so I slowly pulled my hands away from my collarbone. As I did, Akori gasped, and Amahté cursed. Then he called Miu.

She rushed right in, immediately taking control of the situation. "Do not worry, darling, everything is going to be fine. We will figure this out…somehow." She sounded confident enough, but I could see in her face that she was just as lost as I was. How would I ever get any answers if the people helping me didn't know what was going on either?

Still, the three of them eventually managed to calm me down. After many hugs and reassurances, I squeaked out, "What are we going to do? I don't know how to fix this…"

"*You* are going to get some rest," Miu told me. "You have had a very long day. So now you can just go to sleep, and we will try to find out what we can." I nodded; I was so tired…

"How did she manage to do that?" I heard Akori ask Miu at the door.

She ignored him, but I didn't. "I didn't *do* anything!" I protested. Akori looked up, startled.

"How did you hear that?" Miu asked me. I shrugged,

and she stood for a moment, thinking. Then, "Amahté, Akori, why don't you two go and tell your Ab what's happened. I need to speak with Fala." The two looked worried for a moment, but left. I could see them past the door speaking with Khenti.

Miu proceeded to interrogate me about what I could and couldn't see. I told her exactly what I had noticed myself; how both my hearing and my vision were way better than they had ever been before.

Eventually, she nodded, though she was still frowning. She bid me good night and turned to leave. Just as she closed the door behind her, I saw Khenti pull Akori aside. Why would he do that?

I didn't have the energy to puzzle over anything right now; I was just worried about whether or not I could make it to my bed.

I did, but just barely. I was dead to the world before my head hit the pillow.

~*~

The sunlight was what woke me. I buried my face in the pillow and yawned. I still felt too tired to get up. But I couldn't manage to fall back to sleep, so I eventually had to force my eyes to open. The curtains were half open, allowing Ra to shine through. I stood and went to the window, looking out over the grounds.

My head still hurt like crazy, but at least I could focus.

I shook off my early morning stupor, and took a minute to remember what had taken place last night. When I did remember, I groaned; just one more thing that I had to take care of.

I knew I shouldn't complain. I was perfectly healthy, and for the moment I had food and shelter. It just made me kind of angry to know that something like this shouldn't ever have happened, and yet it was happening to *me*.

I laughed harshly, wondering what my Mwt would think of this mess. *"Well, Mwt, your wedding present is a divine item, and it's now more of a tattoo than an amulet. Oh, and I'm courting a demigod, too! But don't worry about it!"* My Mwt probably wouldn't know *what* to think. I doubted that any Mwt had considered this scenario.

"Fala...?" I turned. Akori was standing in the doorway, looking slightly nervous. "Are you alright? Are you feeling better?" He hovered by the door, like he didn't really want to be here.

"Yeah, I'm alright. And I would be even better if you wouldn't use a baby voice with me."

He winced. "I am sorry. You have a concussion, and sometimes that is accompanied by memory loss. I was not sure if you knew where you were." I blinked; I hadn't thought of that. That would have been pretty bad...although then I would have an excuse for punching Khenti in the face.

"No...I'm alright."

Akori finally crossed the room. He leaned back against the railing, then said softly, "Are you feeling any better? You hit your head quite hard." For whatever reason, he wasn't looking at me while he spoke.

"Yeah, I think I'm…mostly alright. A little freaked out, but I'll be okay." I bit my lip, then asked the question that I was most dreading the answer to. "…Akori? Can you tell me what's going on?"

He still wouldn't look at me. "We are not sure. As far as we know right now, this is supposed to happen; it does not change the fact that you are human." I let out a breath that I hadn't known I was holding, and he continued. "My Ab has a theory, but we cannot find any solid evidence."

I snorted. "Yeah, I'll bet he has quite a bit to say about me. Whatever, he's just spouting a bunch of garbage, the lousy—"

"Do not talk about him like that!!"

I started. Akori was finally looking at me, but he looked absolutely *furious*. He had never acted like this, not even when his own Ab had insulted him to his face.

"Akori, calm down. Since when do you care about him?"

"Since right now! You cannot stand there and talk about my Ab like that, it's not right. I will not allow it!" He glowered at me.

I could only stand there, stunned. I couldn't even bring myself to say anything when the door opened again and Amahté walked into the room.

"Hi, you two, what's going on? Did Fala puke again or something?" He paused, obviously expecting one of us to

95

laugh at his teasing. When no one did, he took a closer look around the room. "Uh, what's going on? Really. Akori?" He reached out to place a hand on Akori's shoulder.

Akori yanked his arm away. "What is 'going on' is that Fala was forgetting her place and being very rude to Ab."

"My *place*?" I gasped. "What do you mean 'my place?!'"

Akori didn't miss a beat. "As a human," he told me. "You are not as good as the rest of us. You are not good enough for Amahté, and you do not belong here. So you might as well go home." Amahté and I stared at him, aghast.

"Akori," Amahté whispered, "how can you say such things? You know she's more than good enough for both of us, and she's your friend. You're starting to sound like Ab."

"Well, maybe you should try listening to him too, every once in a while," he snapped. "Then maybe you'd be a good heir for once instead of just some lazy demigod!" Without another word, he turned and stalked out of the room.

"What…was…that?" Amahté choked out.

"I…I don't know. I mean, I'll admit that I insulted Khenti, but he's never seemed to care before." Amahté wasn't looking at me either; he was still staring at the door, as though Akori would come back at any moment. "Amahté…you don't think he was right, do you? About me not belonging here?"

His head snapped up. "No! Of course not. Honestly, I think you would be happy pretty much anywhere. I'd like you to stay with me, but if you want to live in Egypt…it's up to you. But don't worry about 'belonging.'"

I still worried though, even as Amahté pulled me away to breakfast, chattering away about nothing. Akori's statement really cut deep; probably because I had already suspected that I was far too out of place. I belonged back in Egypt, in my simple home, with the Nile rushing past. I didn't belong in the home of a demigod.

And I especially didn't deserve to be courting one.

Chapter Five

Over the next two weeks, things only got worse.

I hardly ever got to spend any time with Amahté; Miu was constantly dragging him away to help her research. We were lucky if we got a few minutes at the end of the day to ourselves, and even that was spoiled by his exhaustion. It was hard to feel wanted when the only person who seemed to want you was falling asleep in the middle of a sentence.

Akori didn't help matters much. He spent his time researching, glaring at me, or generally making me feel unwelcome. I couldn't understand it; he had always seemed so nice.

There were two or three times when I caught Khenti talking to Akori. Each time, Akori had his head lowered submissively, while Khenti spoke to him. Once, Akori talked back, and he got a smack across the face. I tried to find out what was going on, but when the two saw me, Khenti would just sneer and drag Akori away.

"My Ab thinks he might be onto something," Amahté told me one night. "He won't tell us what it is, though. And if Akori knows, he won't say anything."

I shook my head. "I can't understand it. Akori was always so nice; now he's acting more like your Ab every day. He doesn't seem to even mind that he's being treated like a...a tool." I told Amahté about the incidents that I had seen in the hallway between Akori and Khenti. There *had* to be something going on.

Amahté frowned. "That *is* strange. Ab usually doesn't stop to talk to Akori, unless he absolutely has to. And that doesn't happen very often. I wonder—" He was interrupted by the door slamming open. Speak of the demigod: it was Akori.

"Amahté, Ab would like to see you. He is waiting in the library." He turned and left without giving me a passing glance. That stung more than any words he might have said.

Amahté squeezed my hand apologetically. "I guess we should see what he wants," he said. "Maybe he'll tell us what his latest theory is."

I could guess what he wanted. He probably wanted to interrogate me yet again, or convince me to go home *yet again* under the guise of speaking with Amahté. He knew that I would follow, even if I hadn't been asked for. More often than not, Khenti would seek me out just to tell me how out of place I was, or how unsuitable I was for Amahté. I was amazed at the amount of reasons he was able to come up with.

I would never admit it, but he was really starting to get to me. I had felt out of place since the first moment I arrived here; I didn't need anyone to tell me that I didn't belong. Everyone here was too concerned about politics and standing. At home, at least the corruption was outright so I could face it.

Now, Amahté was the only one who would tell me that I did belong. Even Miu had begun to talk to me as little as possible. I was sick of all the prejudice in this place. I just wanted to go home.

"Amahté," I said suddenly, "can I go on ahead? I want to see if I can avoid Khenti." He nodded, and I ran ahead. My statement made perfect sense to him; Khenti would technically be looking for Amahté, not me. But what I really wanted was to catch Khenti alone with Akori, to see if I could hear what was being said. Normally, I wasn't big on eavesdropping, but I needed to know what was going on.

I crept into the library as quietly as possible. It wasn't hard to decide where Khenti was; I could hear him yelling at Akori from the door. If he was trying to be secretive, he wasn't doing a very good job. I snuck as close to them as I dared, peering around a bookshelf.

"—can't even get rid of a lousy human!" Khenti was saying. He looked absolutely livid. I half-expected him to hit Akori again right then.

"Just give me a little more time," Akori pleaded, holding up his hands submissively. "Please, do not do anything to—"

"Hush, you fool!" his Ab snapped. "You have one more day, but after that, I will take matters into my own hands. Now why don't you run along to that *human* while I take care of your mess." Why would he run to me? Was he really going so far out of his way to degrade me?

Akori managed to look both grateful and terrified at the same time. He opened his mouth to say something, and I leaned in closer to hear it.

That was a big mistake. I tripped and fell into the shelf I had been hiding behind. With a huge crash, more than half the books fell to the floor. So much for secrecy. What kind of bookshelf was that unstable? The two demigods turned quickly to look at me, and I held up my hands in surrender.

"Um…Hey Akori, what's going on?" No response. I turned to look at the mess that I had made; it was worse than I thought. I had pretty much managed to empty the bookshelf. "Er, sorry about that. I'll clean it up." I didn't like the idea of doing anything for Khenti, but it *was* my mess. I didn't want to give him another reason to dislike the human race.

To my surprise, Khenti objected. "No, don't bother. I can make *Amisi* pick it up."

"No, I've got it." I didn't want to make Amisi do anything that she didn't have to; she had proved to be a wonderful friend to me. We usually spent time together during the day, if she had spare time between her duties. This wouldn't be fair to her…

"Amisi will get it," Khenti insisted. "After all, she is *only a servant.*" Akori winced, though I couldn't understand why. As far as I knew, he didn't even know Amisi. I was about to say something, but Khenti ushered me into his study before I could get it out. Akori did not follow us.

I had only been in his study once before, and I didn't care for it at all. The whole atmosphere was unfriendly. I had thought that might just be because it belonged to Khenti, but seeing it again changed my mind. It was like the room was designed to make people uncomfortable.

"Now, before Amahté gets here," Khenti said. "I want to make a proposition, human."

"What kind of proposition?" I asked warily. This was a new tactic. He had always been overly forceful with me; now it seemed like he was trying to be reasonable. That could not be a good sign.

"You know you do not belong here," he began, "and don't object, because I know you agree. Amahté probably hasn't told you, but demigods live much longer than humans. The humans in your town live to be about forty years old, correct?" I nodded. "Well, the expected life span for demigods—and that includes Amahté—is about one hundred and fifty years. And none of us will ever look a day over forty."

I was horrified; I hadn't known that. Amahté had mentioned that gods lived much longer than humans, but when he'd said he was just a demigod I had thought we would be alright. Why wouldn't he tell me otherwise?

Amahté was going to outlive me by over one hundred years! That must be why Akori was avoiding me now; he didn't want to get attached to someone with such a comparatively short life span. I couldn't blame him for that...

"So," Khenti continued, "he will stay young in looks, as

well as outliving you by a ridiculous amount. He says he loves you now, but do you really think that he will not move on when you start to age?"

I didn't say anything, because he was right. Amahté would outlive me, *and* he would look young for his whole life. As soon as I hit thirty—if I even made it that far—he was going to meet some other young goddess and forget all about me; after all, even if he was a demigod, he was still a man.

"Um…" I cleared my throat to keep my voice from breaking. "Does this relate to your proposition?" I was pretty sure that it did, but I wouldn't put it past Khenti to bring that up just to make me squirm. I was trying hard not to give him that pleasure.

"Yes, of course it does," he snorted. He knew I was uncomfortable now. "I propose that you go back to your old home in Egypt, and that you take Amisi with you. I know that Amahté lost you your job, so we will provide enough gems to support you until you can get another one."

I couldn't just leave…could I? "What about—"

"Obviously, you will have to take the Osiris amulet with you," he interrupted. "I can give Amisi a charmed bracelet; she can use that to get you back here when needed. She knows how. When we find enough information about the amulet, we can send you a message. That is my proposition."

If I didn't know any better, I would have said that he was trying to be nice, trying to give me my life back. But the look in his eyes said otherwise; I knew that he just wanted me gone, and for some reason he wanted Amisi gone, too. And he wanted to break me before I left.

Normally, I would have disagreed to this right away. I couldn't be sure if Khenti was telling the truth—he was so set on being rid of me, I knew he would say anything to make me leave. But if what he said was true, then I was hurting both Akori and Amahté without even realizing it. That wasn't right.

"Fala?" Ah, Amahté was finally here. What had taken him so long? "What are you doing here with Ab?"

I took a deep breath and turned to him. "Amahté, if I ask you something, do you promise to answer honestly?" I needed to know the truth.

"Wha-? Of course, but—"

"Just answer me this: how long does a demigod live?"

The room grew dead silent. I could practically hear Khenti's smirk—he was getting what he wanted. I could also tell that he didn't want to answer my question, but there was no way that he was getting out of this one. I would simply stare at him until he gave me an answer.

It didn't take long. Amahté was not a very patient person. "We-ell…usually somewhere around…a hundred and fifty years…"

"And *when* were you planning on telling me this?" I demanded angrily. "When were you planning on telling me that you were going to stay young, and outlive me by over a hundred years?! Even the pharaoh does not live nearly that long!" He flinched, and I turned to Khenti. "Fine. I accept.

When can I leave?" I couldn't be around any of them right now. He had lied to me, had used me—!

Amahté looked horrified, but he would get over it in fifty years or so.

The twins' Ab grinned; this was obviously the outcome he had been hoping for. I was too upset to care. "You can leave as soon as you've packed," he told me. I nodded; I was already halfway out the door.

Amahté followed me as I went to my room. "But, Fala, why are you leaving? I really, really want you to stay, and the last time I checked, you wanted to stay, too."

I turned on him. "The last time you checked, I wasn't aware of the fact that you're going to look young for almost two centuries, while I get old and crippled and *die*!!" I didn't wait for a response. I just slammed the door in his face and started packing.

By the time I finished packing, it was well past midnight. I left my things out and collapsed into bed. It had been an extremely tiring day.

~*~

Despite my lack of sleep, I woke early. I was so uncomfortable. I was so hot... I lay still for a few moments, but quickly realized that I wasn't going to fall back to sleep. I opened my eyes...and discovered that I was back at home, in Egypt.

No wonder I was so uncomfortable; I had grown used to the cushy beds at the twins' estate. And it was so much cooler there. I would have to get used to my home all over again.

I sat up and looked around; all of my things were there, just as I had packed them. There was one small knapsack sitting next to my pillow; when I opened it, I found that it was filled to the brim with precious gems. Well, bartering wasn't going to be a problem anytime soon. Hopefully these wouldn't get stolen.

I got out of bed and dressed quickly. Then, I went to make myself breakfast, only to find that Amisi had beaten me to it. In my own kitchen. I was puzzled, but then I remembered that part of Khenti's proposition had been that Amisi would come home with me.

I snorted bitterly. Proposition, my ass. He just wanted to get rid of me so he could go back to bossing around humans that *wouldn't* mouth off to him.

Amisi heard me and turned around. "Good morning, sleepyhead," she said. Her tone was cheerful, but it seemed forced, and the smile on her face didn't reach her eyes. They were red, as though she had been crying. I went to her and put my hand on her shoulder.

"Are you alright? You look like you've been crying." She was my only friend here now. I wanted to do what I could to make her happy.

She went on as if she hadn't heard me. "I whipped up some bread for breakfast; I hope you do not mind. And I went out and got a few extra ingredients for lunch."

"Amisi—"

But she just kept talking. What didn't she want to talk about? "Oh, I also tidied up a bit while you were asleep. The place was not exactly clean, in fact it looked like someone had been digging through your things." This caught my attention. I didn't own much, but I always made sure that my house was clean.

"Did you finish cleaning it up?" I asked sharply.

Amisi looked up, startled. "N-No, I did not really get the chance. I just cleaned up a little, and then I started making breakfast. Most of the living room is still a mess…" I was gone before she had finished speaking, running into my living room.

She was right; it was a mess. I never let my house get nearly this dirty, not even when someone was boarding here. I dug through what was left of my belongings, searching for the two that were most precious to me.

When I found them, I nearly cried. "Mwt…"

My Mwt's wedding dress was at the very bottom of the pile, torn to shreds. It was barely recognizable as anything other than a rag. Right next to it was a torn, crumpled, ripped up piece of paper that I knew to be my Mwt's letter to me. She had written it when I was four years old, when I had stayed with an aunt for a short period of time. I had always read that when I needed strength. Now it was gone.

How had anyone even gotten to them? The twins had told me—no, had *promised* me that no human could get through their barrier. I thought briefly of Akori; had he distanced himself from me so much, so quickly? I couldn't be sure that the answer to that was no.

Behind me, Amisi murmured, "Fala, I am so sorry...I did not think. I did not realize that anything that was...destroyed might have been important to you. I thought it would have been kept with you..."

"Well, they were," I choked out. "That's all I had left of my Mwt, and somebody destroyed them!" Now I was angry. How dare someone do this? What had I ever done to deserve all this? "I'm going for a walk," I announced, standing quickly. "If I find out who did this, you might need to help me bury a body."

I left the house as fast as I could, ignoring her sputters. I was too angry to think clearly right now, and if I stayed to talk to her, I would say something that I would regret later.

I took a deep breath outside the house, composing myself. As much as I wished otherwise, I couldn't do anything about it. I had no way of knowing who had invaded my home.

After I had calmed down a little bit, I began to walk to the fountain in the center of town. I could think freely there, I hoped. Usually, as an outcast, I went unnoticed in a crowd. This time, however, it seemed like everyone stopped what they were doing to look at me. That was unusual, to say the least.

"Um...hi, everyone." No one answered me, and there was some snickering from the crowd. I took a step forward, confused, and the people reacted without a second thought. They backed away from me, and a few Mwts pulled their children behind them. "What is going on?" I asked. They were treating me like some sort of leper.

"You've been found out, you demon!" someone finally shouted.

My cheeks flushed once more with anger. "And just what is *that* supposed to mean?!" I had no idea what was going on, and nobody seemed willing to help me. I rushed home, my cheeks burning. 'It's probably just some stupid rumor,' I told myself. 'Things will get better in time.'

The next day, I went to try and find a job. With Amisi taking care of the house—mostly before I even woke, no matter how hard I tried—I really wanted to have something to do. Khenti *had* sent gems, it was true, but I didn't want to have to rely on him. It would be nice to be able to depend on myself.

When I first left the house, I tripped over a log someone had left, face-first into a pile of dung. I should have seen that as an omen and stayed inside.

I couldn't go back to my old position, that was for sure. I thought that maybe I would be able to find a job working in the marketplace; I could transport or sort goods, a simple enough task that would give decent pay.

"Hello, sir," I said politely to the first vendor I saw. He was old and wizened, and he certainly looked like he could use the help.

He turned, saw who I was, and spit in my face.

The rest of the day went much the same way. Why was this happening? I returned home feeling downcast and defeated.

"Do not worry, Fala," said Amisi, trying to cheer me up. "Sometimes, good things only come with time and patience. I am sure that at some point things will begin to get better."

Amisi was wrong; nothing improved. Instead of treating me like an outcast, the townsfolk treated me like a demon. I was cursed at, laughed at, and things were thrown at me on a regular basis. It turned out that my sudden 'vanishing act,' combined with my mysterious reappearance, had convinced the people that I was some sort of witch.

That meant that I couldn't get a job. I was forced to turn to the gems that Khenti had given to me. I had no idea what each of them was worth, so the first day I headed out after grabbing some at random.

The vendors, thankfully, were greedy. I found one especially greasy little man who had everything I needed. He gladly took the gems; as long as I had money, he didn't care what the rumors said about me. I was able to buy a good portion of wheat and some fruit and meat for the day. Despite the previous day's failure, I was happy with today's success.

That is, until I told Amisi what I had done. "Fala," she wailed, "why did you not take me with you?"

"I didn't want to bother you!" I said. She was working so hard as it was—I hadn't wanted to add anything to her already-full plate.

"Bother me next time!" she said. "You could have

gotten more than twice that for the gems you took!"

My mouth fell open. They had been worth that much? That vendor had tricked me! I gritted my teeth, ashamed, and promised to ask Amisi first just how much I should get for each gem.

Although they helped me pay for my necessities, the gems didn't really help my situation. Everyone was convinced that I had used my 'dark powers' to steal them from the pharaoh. I couldn't even blame them for being suspicious: I had no job, no spouse and no inheritance. My having anything to barter with made no sense at all.

Several times, I came home to a house covered in rotting fruit.

Amisi was no help, though she tried to be. She cooked much better than I ever could, and she helped me to clean. But every time I mentioned Akori, she would flinch away and start babbling on about nothing.

I came home from a particularly bad day about a month later. Some of the younger kids had decided that the rotten fruit no longer belonged on my *house*, but on me. I had dodged them as best I could, but a few tomatoes had hit me.

I went straight to the kitchen to wash it off. Right then I didn't care that the water basin had been filled for that night's dinner; I just wanted to get myself clean. Even putting up with Khenti had been better than this!

"Damn little kids," I muttered, "throwing stuff at me like that. My tunic is probably ruined; I'll have to dye the whole thing just to make it one color again. Damn Khenti and his stupid prejudice for driving me here. He probably knew that the town thinks I'm a freaking demon…he probably set me up…" I finished scrubbing the remains of the fruit off my skin; most of it had hit my tunic, which I could wash later. I threw down the rag I'd been using with one final curse: "Damn Akori for turning his back on me!"

"Do not say that!!" I turned, startled. Amisi was standing in the doorway, the tears I had seen in her eyes for days streaming down her cheeks. "Do not ever speak about Akori that way!"

"Why not? It's true," I countered. My surprise had taken the edge off of my initial anger, but I was still so angry—I had every right to be!

"No it is not!" she insisted. "Akori saved the both of us, he—" She broke off, putting both hands over her mouth.

"He what?" I demanded. "How has he saved us? He's *doomed* us, that's what he's done! He abandoned the both of us, and now we're being left here to rot!"

I stood, chest heaving, waiting for her response. But she only continued to sob.

"Amisi, what were you going to say?!" She shook her head, still crying, still covering her face with her hands. I went over to her, put my hands on her shoulders, and forced her to look at me. "Tell me. *Now.*" I knew I shouldn't force her like this, but I needed to know. If Akori really *hadn't* abandoned us, if there was a reason…

"K-Khenti m-made him," she finally sobbed, letting her

hands drop weakly to her chest. "He s-said that if Akor-ri d-did not get us to l-leave, he would k-kill us! He would not d-do that to his f-f-friends!" She totally broke down then, and I held her close.

As horrible as it was, I felt my anger fade. I was actually *glad* that that was what had happened. I was glad that I could still trust Akori.

But something didn't make sense. "Amisi," I said gently, "why did you have to come, too? I could have gotten back if the charm had been explained to me." She couldn't just be here to help me with that. I mean, as far as I could tell, it was just the little bracelet that Amisi always wore around her wrist. One of them, anyway. How hard could that be to learn?

She buried her face in my shoulder. "...Because *he* d-did not like that" —she hiccupped—"Akori and I were t-together..."

I pulled her back so that I could look her in the eye. "Really? You and Akori are together? I didn't know he was courting you." They were so perfect for each other! They were both so quiet and kind and polite...but I hadn't even known that they had met properly.

Amisi nodded shyly. "W-We have been seeing each other for-hic- a while...but Khenti found out the night you g-got hu-ur-t."

"Amisi..."

"I d-did not mean to give us away," she sobbed, "but I saw everyone had gathered and—and—I thought the worst!

I thought Khenti had tried to get rid of Akori again!"

"Oh…it's alright, Amisi. Everything will be okay." This wasn't how I would have wanted to find out…but I was glad that she and Akori had each other. I had been worried that, while Amahté and I were off together, he had been lonely. Now I knew that that wasn't the case.

Now I also knew that I hated Khenti more than I had ever thought it possible to hate anyone. And if he wanted me to stay here, then there was no way that I was going to stay. What did I have to lose? Everyone already thought that I was a demon—I would have to leave soon anyway if I didn't want to risk them coming after me.

"Why didn't you want to tell me that?" I asked her. "We could've gone back sooner, or we could have not left at all. We could have stayed."

She sniffed, drying her eyes. "Khenti said that if I t-told you, he would hurt you."

"Is that all?" I scoffed. "I can handle one egocentric demigod, Amisi. Don't worry about it." At least, I hoped that I could; I wasn't really sure. I wouldn't go down without a fight, though. "Amisi…if you don't mind…I'd really like to go back and be with Amahté. I don't know if that's okay with you, but—oof!" Amisi had, in her haste, practically tackled me. I took that as a yes.

We headed out as soon as we had packed our things. It didn't take long; each of us only had about enough to fill a knapsack. The rest of our things had been vandalized or stolen long ago.

Since I had no idea of where we were going, I just followed Amisi's lead. She led us to a shrine, one on the very edge of town. As we entered, I read the symbols on the door; it was a shrine to all demigods. Huh. I guess that would explain why we were here.

Amisi sat at the altar. When I asked what she was doing, she said she had to focus; otherwise, we could end up at any demigod's house. I cringed at that, thinking of all the demigods I had met at the gala. I certainly wouldn't want to depend on any of them.

Not long after that, she told me not to talk to her, because she had to recite a spell. I didn't know much about magic, but I did know that a single syllable could mean the difference between a healing and destruction.

"Hey, what are you two ruffians doing here?" Oh, wonderful. Just what we needed: three priests and their guards. I glanced at Amisi, willing her to go faster, but too afraid of messing her up to say anything. One of the guards ran up and grabbed my arm. I tried pushing him away, but he was stronger than me. He shouldn't be stronger than me, I should be able to do this—!

"This crime against the gods will not go unpunished," intoned a priest. "You must be turned over to the people!"

I struggled even harder, panicking now. This just got better and better, didn't it? Being 'turned over to the people' *sounded* nice and fair, but it wasn't. Unless the person managed extreme bribery, the 'criminal' was usually burnt at the stake, or pulled apart by horses…something like that.

Amisi's eyes snapped open. "I am done, Fala! Quickly, take my hand!" I kicked the guard in the chest with all the force I could muster, sending him reeling back. Then I grabbed Amisi's wrist, praying that it had worked.

"...Fala...? Fala?" I opened my eyes, and released the breath I had been holding; we were in my room in Khenti's estate. I never thought I would think so, but it had never seemed so welcome.

"I guess it worked," I told Amisi, laughing a little. "I was a little worried when those guys showed up. We almost didn't make it!" We both laughed at that; we could afford to now, since we didn't have to worry about it anymore. "Now I just have to find Khenti so I can kick his—"

"Fala! You're back!" Before I had a chance to turn, Amahté's strong arms were around me. "Oh, gods, I'm so glad; I thought you were really gone! I thought you had really left for good!"

"Can't...breathe..." I choked out. He let go, and I gasped for breath (for dramatic effect).

"Why did you decide to come back?" He was so happy, I almost didn't want to tell him what his Ab had done. He had to know, though—he deserved to know what had been going on with his brother.

"It's...a long story," I said slowly. "And it all goes back to your Ab."

The smile faded from his face. "...What's he done now?" he asked, sounding defeated.

"Khenti...threatened Amisi and me to get to Akori. He

told your brother that if he didn't try to get rid of me, then I would be killed."

Realization dawned on his face. "That's why he was sounding like Ab," he whispered. "He was trying to scare you away so you wouldn't get hurt."

"Yes. I just found out about it—Amisi told me. That's why we came back."

He shook his head in disgust, but I could see that this information didn't surprise him. I wondered how many schemes Khenti had tried to pull off in the past.

"Um..." Amisi was nervously fingering her charmed bracelet. She was glancing nervously past us, probably thinking of Akori. Did she not want to go alone...?

"So," I asked Amahté, "where's Akori? I need to talk to him about something important."

His face fell. "He...He's in his room. He hasn't been doing so well; I'm really worried about him." Amisi gasped, but he didn't seem to notice. "Ever since you left, he hasn't been eating properly, and every time he tries to sleep he has nightmares. And he doesn't try to do *anything*. He just sits around."

"Have you talked to him at all?"

Amahté shrugged helplessly. "I tried a few times, but he just...stared right through me, like he didn't even know I was there. Do you think you can talk to him? Please? He probably feels guilty, I'm sure seeing you will help."

"I'll talk to him," I promised, although I was sure that I wasn't the only one he wanted to see. "Why don't we go see him now?" Amahté nodded, and we followed him out the door. Amisi seemed to know where she was going, but I had no clue; I had only been to Akori's room once.

When we reached Akori's room, Amisi went in first. Amahté tried to stop her—I hadn't told him about Amisi's relationship with Akori—but I told him to let her through. A moment later, though, she was crying again, and I wondered if it was right to bring her here.

The room was nearly pitch black; the only light came from the doorway and a bedside candle. Even though he was asleep, I could see how strained Akori was. His brow was furrowed, and there were tearstains on his cheeks. Amisi was already kneeling at his side, shaking him.

"Akori?" she whispered fearfully. "Akori, please wake up!"

For one wild moment, I thought that we were too late, that he wouldn't wake. But that was ridiculous—you couldn't die from a broken heart.

He stirred, and his eyes slowly opened. When he saw the three of us, his eyes widened, and he sat up. "I am dreaming," he muttered, shaking his head. "I must be dreaming. You...you both went back to Egypt. You both left..."

"You are awake," Amisi assured him gently. "We came back. Egypt was not so impressive."

Akori shook his head slowly. "But...Fala would hate me now. She would not know...she would not come back..."

"Akori!" His head snapped up to meet my gaze. "You

are awake, and I *do* know. Amisi told me. If you still think you're dreaming, I would be more than happy to pinch you, or whatever it takes to show you that you're awake." And with that, I reached over and slapped his arm…probably a little harder than necessary. "You should have said something, Akori. We would have helped you."

"Ouch!" He pulled away, then laughed softly. "I…I suppose I really am awake, huh?"

"And making a complete fool of yourself," Amisi told him. He blushed, but he didn't get the chance to say anything. Amisi was suddenly occupying his lips. He didn't object; he just pulled her closer to him.

"Whoa! When did this happen?" Amahté exclaimed.

I shrugged. "Ah…apparently, it's been going on for a while."

"What? And I didn't know? That's just wrong." I rolled my eyes, but I didn't get a chance to be sarcastic. Amahté made sure of that with a kiss.

I smiled at him when he pulled away. "Okay, okay. Everyone is together now, we can all be happy again. Now can we eat? I'm starving." Everyone laughed at that, but they agreed. We headed for the kitchen; Akori had his arm around Amisi's shoulders, and Amahté and I were holding hands.

For once, things felt normal, or at least as normal as they could get. It was nice, the companionship we all shared. I had missed Egypt before, but now that I had spent some time away from the twins I knew it wasn't worth it. I would much rather feel a little out of place than feel lonely or abandoned. And besides, I was sure I would adjust.

Of course, then we just *had* to run into Khenti. He stopped dead in his tracks, a look of shock on his face. Then he composed himself and sneered at us: "What are you two doing back?" He turned to Akori. "You know what this means, do you not? Or are you so stupid that you forgot our bargain?"

"Ab, Fala is *my* guest," Amahté interjected. "She has every right to be here. And as for Amisi, she has been working here for her whole life; we've no right to make her leave. You can't manipulate someone by using their friends' lives as ransom."

"Be quiet! Amahté, I have *every* right. This is my property, and I will do with it as I please. And you—" he glared at me— "seem to have forgotten our little conversation. Amahté's life will be almost four times as long as yours; do you think that that fact can be ignored?"

I took a deep breath to calm myself. If I let my emotions get the better of me, I would lose. "That *is* certainly a problem," I admitted, "but Amahté and I can work around it. As can Amisi and Akori, I'm sure." I moved to step around him, but he grabbed my arm. "Let go of me!"

"Not a chance! I'm going to spell-bind you so tightly you won't even remember your own name!" I felt something touch me. Not physically—I already knew he was touching my arm. It was like there was something in my head, coming closer and closer until—

It felt like someone was *burning* me… I tried to pull away, but his grip was too strong. After what seemed like an eternity (but was probably only a few seconds), I realized that I couldn't win this time. Whatever horrible thing he was planning to do to me, I wasn't strong enough to stop it.

Just as I started to give up, I felt a sharp pain in my head. The same one that I had felt when Khenti had tried to take the amulet from me. I stayed conscious long enough to think, 'I wonder what will happen now…'

Then the darkness overtook me.

~*~

When I woke, the first thing that I noticed was that I was lying on my stomach. I *never* fell asleep like that. I pushed myself up into a sitting position, looking around. I felt a small tug at my shoulder-blades, but I wrote it off as knots. I had been so stressed lately, after all.

I was back in my room, but I wasn't alone. Amahté was standing at the door. It looked like he was arguing with someone, but I couldn't see who it was. Why in Ra's name would he be arguing with someone? Was something wrong?

The argument got louder, and I recognized Khenti's voice. "She cannot stay here, there is no way!" he was saying. "She's a menace, and we don't even know what she is. Just look at her!"

"That's exactly why she *can* stay here, Ab," Amahté retorted. "If we end up finding out that Fala is related to someone important, do you want to explain to them why she was sent back to Egypt? Or if something happens to her and the amulet, do you want to be the one to explain to Osiris why it is lost?"

Wait, they were talking about me? How come they didn't know what I was? My heart sank; if *they* didn't know what I was, then there was no way I was human.

That didn't seem fair at all. I knew so many people even in my small town who said constantly that they wanted to have the power of the gods, that they would do anything to become like the gods. I had been perfectly happy the way I was. Yes, I wanted to move…but I would have been fine there if I had to be.

Why was this happening to me?

Khenti still hadn't responded to Amahté's question. It seemed like he didn't have an argument for Amahté's logic— that scared me a little. For once, I sincerely hoped he was wrong. Amahté seemed pretty confident, though, and he continued to talk. "I didn't think so. Now, if you will kindly excuse me, I am going to check on her." With that, he shut the door in Khenti's face, and turned to face me. "Oh, you're awake."

I nodded, biting my lip. "Amahté… was he being serious? When he said that he didn't know what I was?"

"…You heard that?" Another nod. "Well… yeah, he was being serious. I really am sorry, Fala. I promise, I'll try to find out what's going on as soon as I can. I don't know if my Mwt will want to help—she'll probably take my Ab's side at this point—but I know we can count on Akori."

"What makes you so sure that I'm not human?" I knew that he probably had his reasons, but if I didn't know them, I could still argue that I was human. And even if I couldn't, I had the right to know.

He frowned. "My Mwt didn't tell you? Your senses, for one thing. The way you see and hear things is at least as advanced as the senses of a demigod, if not more. That happened awhile ago, when the amulet went into your chest. And, um…"

"'Um?' What's 'um?'" He just shook his head. I sighed, and moved to stand up.

"What are you doing?" Amahté demanded.

I rolled my eyes at him. "What does it look like I'm doing? I'm getting out of bed; I want to change my tunic. And afterwards, I want to eat and actually *do* something, instead of just sitting around. I need to start getting more exercise."

When I had been working as a farmhand, I had gotten more than enough exercise. I had been strong enough to take care of myself. But a month of living here and being pampered had definitely taken its toll on my physical ability. I just hadn't noticed it until that guard had been able to keep his hold on me. That was something that I couldn't allow.

I stood up and crossed the room, planning to go straight to the dresser and its warmer contents—I had to readjust to the cooler temperatures all over again. But I didn't get that far. Because to get to the dresser, I had to walk by a full-length mirror; once I saw my reflection, I *had* to stop and take a closer look.

I was pretty sure that I knew what Amahté had been about to say. *And, um... Fala, you have wings. But don't worry about it.*

They weren't dragon wings, like Amahté and Akori had. They were more like a bird's wings. Huge, pure-white bird's wings that were sticking out of my shoulder blades. I slumped to the floor. I guess they were right; I *couldn't* be human. Last time I checked, humans didn't have wings of any sort.

Oh sweet Isis, Mwt of all things…

I took a deep breath. Okay. This was alright. Even though this was, once again, getting much too strange for me, nothing really surprised me anymore. The pharaoh could turn out to be some strange species of demigod that planned on eating us all, and it wouldn't affect me. So this was no big deal. I *would not* freak out. Everything would be fine…

Oh dear Ra, who was I kidding? This was not fine! This was not okay, not at all—I mean, I had *wings*, for crying out loud! I started hyperventilating.

Amahté stuck his head into the hall, called for Akori, and then ran over to me. "Don't worry, Fala, it's okay!" he tried to assure me. "Everything will be alright, it's not such a big deal!"

"Amahté is right, Fala," Akori added. I jumped; I had been focusing so hard on Amahté that I hadn't heard him come sit beside me. "I am sorry, I did not mean to scare you. Please calm down…"

The two of them spent the next ten minutes trying to calm me down. Somehow, they finally managed. When they did, I stood up with my back to the mirror, trying to see my backside. It was hard; my new wings kept getting in the way. They kept turning the same way I did, keeping me from what I wanted to check. The wings were just too big; if I did have a tail, I couldn't see it. It didn't *feel* like I had a tail, but at this point, I just couldn't be sure.

"Fala…do you mind if I ask what it is you are doing?" Akori asked me.

"Checking for a tail," I admitted, finally giving up and sitting down again. I could feel my wings automatically fold behind me. It was strange—even though they were new, it didn't seem like I was having any trouble with them. They just…went with my body. I didn't even really have to think about it.

The brothers looked at each other, then burst out laughing. I scowled at them—that was nice, laugh at the panicking one. That's a great help.

"You don't have a tail!" Amahté gasped. "What gave you that idea?" I punched his shoulder. Akori got the message; he managed to get himself under control. But Amahté just kept laughing, so I took a pillow from the bed and stuck it in his mouth.

"Bleh! Gross, Fala," he complained.

I shrugged. "Well, that's what you get for laughing at me. So there." I knew it wasn't very mature to do it, but I still stuck my tongue out at him. Then I sighed. "This is going to complicate my wardrobe. I'm going to have to put slits in the back of all my clothes!"

"No, you do not," Akori told me. He stood with me (Amahté couldn't; he was still giggling helplessly on the floor). "Amisi had said that she had seen some clothes she thought you might like; she should be back any moment. Wearing those clothes will be much easier than trying to alter your whole wardrobe, I can assure you. Ah, here she is," he added as Amisi walked through the door.

She smiled at me, shifting the basket in her arms. "Hello, Fala. I am so glad that you are awake. I managed to find some clothes for you—I hope that they are to your liking." I smiled back and accepted the clothes, but I cringed internally. How was I going to get the clothes I was wearing off? They wouldn't fit over my new wings. Amisi must have foreseen this problem, because she said, "I have brought a small knife with me. If you like, I can go with you and cut your tunic off." Frowning, she added, "Of course, that would ruin the tunic…"

"That's okay. It's already ruined, anyway." It was the same tunic that I had been wearing when those kids had thrown stuff at me; I had been so excited about seeing the twins again that I had forgotten to change out of it. "Do you mind helping me?" I asked.

"No, not at all," she beamed. Akori scowled at her. "He has been trying to get me to do less work," she explained, "but I do not even work that much, not anymore. Only when I cannot be with him. And I like it; it is something for me to do, that keeps me in shape." She giggled as Akori pulled her close to give her a kiss on the cheek.

"But I do not like you doing all of the work," Akori murmured, still holding her. "You do not have to anymore; you are no longer a servant. You should let someone else do the work for you."

Amisi shrugged. "'Old habits die hard,'" she quoted, "and also, Fala likes to take care of herself just as much as I do. Now I must go help her get that tunic off." With another kiss, she pulled away from Akori, and pulled me into the washroom. I turned around so she could cut my tunic off.

"What did Akori mean back there? Did Khenti agree to let you go?" I doubted it, but Akori had said that she was no longer a servant. Had Akori or Amahté bribed him into freeing her?

"Oh, yes, only because he had to," she explained. "Amahté found an old document in the library. By accident, of course; he did not know that we were together at the time. But the document stated that, if a godling, demigod, god, or High God courts a human, then that human cannot be owned. So, because Akori is courting me, Khenti had to let me go."

"How long ago did you find this out?"

"It was a while ago now…I do believe it was shortly after you arrived here, Fala."

"Why wait so long?" If I had been in her position, I would have slapped that document in Khenti's face the first chance I got.

"I was not sure if I wanted to be free," she said softly. "I have been a servant of this house for my entire life; I have never known anything else. It is frightening, not knowing where you will go or what you will do for a living. We only took action now because we had to; Master Khenti was going to sell me to another demigod. Akori and I would have been separated for good..."

I hadn't looked at it that way. I couldn't imagine being so indebted to someone that you were *afraid* to be free. But it was done now—I was happy for Amisi. Khenti couldn't boss her around anymore and she and Akori would be together.

We stood in silence for a few minutes. Finally, Amisi said, "There, it is done." She finished cutting my tunic off and went to leave.

"Amisi?" I called. "If you are free, I think you should do less work, too. If you keep doing work, Khenti will still see you as a servant, and you're not. So...I think you should listen to Akori." I grinned. "We can spend time together, I'll take care of you."

She bit her lip. "I will try...but I am so used to being a servant. It will be a while before I know what to do with myself." And with that, she left.

I turned to the basket of clothes that I had been given, pulling things out one by one. All the tunics were clearly made to go with wings; they were low-backed, so my wings could go around them instead of through them.

I chose one at random. Amisi had gotten used to my

taste in clothes, so she had picked simple ones. It took me a few minutes to get the tunic on, and I pulled out quite a few feathers. That hurt really badly; it was like pulling out all my hair, again and again. I hadn't expected that.

I finally got it on. I just pulled simple leggings on underneath; I didn't want to worry about those right now. Plus, most of the leggings were either black or dark brown.

When I finally stepped out of the washroom, Amahté whistled. "Wow, Fala. That looks really good on you." I looked down to see what tunic I had chosen. It was very simple, just how I liked it. There were two ties to hold it up: one that looped around the back of my neck, and another that tied below my shoulder blades, out of the way of my wings. The fabric was very soft (probably silk or something), and the whole thing was a beautiful golden color. The leggings were plain black.

Amisi laughed, saying, "I am so very glad that you picked that one. It is my favorite." Personally, I was just glad that I matched, seeing how I had picked my clothes completely at random. I probably should stop doing that...

Amahté came up to me, and went around to my back. "Fala," he scolded me, "you're feathers are all ruffled." I had expected that; I had pulled a lot out. Amahté started straightening out my feathers, making me jump—I hadn't thought that my new wings would be so sensitive to both pain *and* pleasure.

Akori chuckled. "Perhaps now we could all go flying together," he suggested.

I tensed. "Akori," Amahté complained, "I just got her to calm down! You messed up all my hard work. Geez, these kinds of wings are so much harder to take care of. You should—"

"Speaking of wings," I interrupted, "is there any particular reason why I have them? Since I'm assuming it's not normal." When was anything normal with me?

"It is certainly not normal," Akori told me cheerfully. "And we are not exactly sure of why you have them." He turned to Amahté. "Perhaps there is something in the library."

I shook my head. "Your Mwt has been looking through the library almost non-stop. She would have found something by now, right?"

"Not necessarily. The library is huge—you've seen it. Mwt has been working her way through, but she can only move so quickly. She has not been through most of the library."

"Alright then. Let's go." I glanced around to see if Amisi would come, too, but she had left.

The twins just looked at me blankly. "Go where?" Amahté asked.

"To the library," I deadpanned. "We're going to help your Mwt. The sooner we get through the information we have, the sooner we'll get answers." Or at least that was my hope. I couldn't know for sure, but it seemed like there had to be something there. Why else would Miu spend so much time looking?

I didn't wait for the twins to head off; they would follow me, eventually. And they did, albeit hesitantly. They seemed to think that the library wouldn't be of any help.

"Fala," Akori said, "do you not think that someone would have noticed if there was a crucial piece of evidence? It is true that Mwt has not been through everything, but she *has* been through most of the official documents and records."

"That's not what I want to look at. There has to be something somewhere else. Maybe an informal record, maybe some notes scribbled on the back of a scroll. That's where we'll find what we need." I was sure of it. That was always where the most important things were, in the last place people looked. Miu was already checking the 'normal' stuff; I just needed to go straight to the things no one looked at.

Thankfully, the library was not very far from my room. "You two can go to either side," I told them. "I'll go straight to the back. We can meet back here just before lunch." Amahté and Akori nodded and headed off in their separate directions.

The first thing I did was look for the section covered in the most dust. It wasn't very hard to find—I turned a corner and was practically choking on the stuff. I coughed and instinctively shook out my wings.

There were so many untouched scrolls back here! Surely one of them could help me. I reached for the nearest one and unrolled it. It was about an uprising in the human world that the gods were considering interfering in. Well, that wasn't helpful at all. I pulled one from a higher shelf across the aisle. This was about a famine.

This might take longer than I had first thought.

It didn't take me long, though, to figure out what the sections were about. And soon enough I had located the section on the history of the realm of the gods. I combed through scroll after scroll about Ra, Isis, Set…Osiris! Finally!

I pulled down the scroll and opened it eagerly. As I read though, I slowed. This didn't have the answers I was searching for, but it still seemed important. I sat down in the dust and read it again, more thoroughly this time.

'Osiris was born to two gods,' it read, 'and raised to become one of them. It was fully expected that he would one day marry Isis, a girl destined to become a goddess.

'He began courting her, just as he was instructed, on the night he turned seventeen. They had been childhood friends, so cooperating with an arranged marriage wasn't difficult. Everything seemed to be going according to plan; the wedding was set for shortly after Osiris' eighteenth birthday. However, as that date drew nearer, Osiris began to see Isis less and less. He cancelled visits to her family, and when he did agree to meet with her, he was not nearly as attentive as he usually was. Eventually Isis stopped trying to see him. Those close to her said that her relationship with him became mere companionship, whereas before it had been romance.

'Their families, of course, said nothing; the wedding

would proceed as planned. But six weeks before his eighteenth birthday, six weeks before he would become a full god, he vanished. This sent things into chaos, of course. Osiris could not become a god if he did not attend this ceremony. His family's status would be lost. Then, just one week before the ceremony, they found him. But he wasn't alone, nor was he with a goddess. He was with a human woman. The parents tried to deny that she had anything to do with their son, but all their power couldn't hide the way he acted around her. And when they tried to send her away, Osiris revealed the truth: the two had been married, bound by vows of Ra. No god could break those vows.

'So they were forced to allow her to stay. Osiris did become a true god. When they realized that he was a High God, one of the thirteen most powerful gods, his parents banished themselves. And thus, Osiris became the ruler of both the Land of the Dead and all that had been his Ab's. But that power came at a price. As a High God, Osiris could only visit Egypt once each year; otherwise, he was bound to the realm of the gods. There were other laws, of course, but this was the most taxing; his wife was still human, and in love with both him and the human world. While the couple deliberated, a child was born, only adding to the strife. No one knew what this child, a half-god, was capable of.

'In the end, though, the child was the deciding factor. Osiris knew the standards and troubles that would await his child if she remained with him, and it could not go back alone. Both the child and its Mwt were to go back to the human realm, to live out their days without Osiris' presence. It was also agreed that the child would not know who its Ab was. While both parents accepted this, Osiris felt as though he bore the most responsibility. In apology to his wife, he gave her a single amulet. An amulet powerful enough to protect both her and the child. She accepted his gift, and left for the human world. And with her, the Osiris amulet vanished.'

I finished reading and leaned back against the shelf with a huff. Amahté and his family were wrong—the amulet hadn't been stolen from Osiris! The wife had taken it with her. And it wasn't simply a gift, as I had been told, but something made to protect her.

Somewhere between the Mwt and the child, the amulet might have gotten stolen, but to me it just sounded like it had been lost. We just had to find the child.

I stood, satisfied with my work, and brought the scroll back to our meeting-place. Amahté was already there, and we didn't have to wait long before Akori showed up.

"Did either of you find anything?" I asked. Both of them shook their heads. "I found this. It sounds pretty important."

I showed them the scroll, and they read it over. Akori finished reading before Amahté did. "I was not even aware that there was a child," he said. "That could change everything, especially if the amulet did travel to the human world with the wife and child."

"It sounds almost like it was just...lost," Amahté added, finally done.

"That's what I thought. And if it was simply lost, then that would explain why the amulet is 'confused', right?"

"That would make sense," Akori said slowly. "If it was lost, then it may have been actively searching for a new family to protect in order to fulfill its purpose. You would have allowed that, so the amulet bonded to you and your Mwt in place of the rightful heirs."

"Is there any way to know for sure?" All of this guessing was fine, but I wanted a way to know for sure.

"Perhaps we should go ask Seer about it."

"Seer? What's that?" I asked nervously.

"Not what, who. Seer is one of our Mwt's associates. She is a bit like an oracle, but she is much more specific."

"So…she uses people's palms and things like that?"

"Nope," said Amahté. "She can't; Seer is blind." This bit of information baffled me. She was blind, and they called her Seer? That made no sense at all. Sometimes I thought that demigods spent their time coming up with ways to confuse the rest of us.

Wait…if Seer was psychic, then… "Why didn't we go to her to figure out who the amulet belongs to? Wouldn't that be easier?"

Akori shrugged. "She cannot see *everything*," he said, "and we had already asked her. She informed us that she would not be able to do anything about it, because her powers mostly focus on using people, not objects, to get information."

"Oh, okay… how long will you be gone?" I questioned.

As ridiculous as it sounded, I really didn't want to be alone just then. Not with everything that had happened recently.

"It won't take long," Amahté said. "*We* will be back before dinnertime; you're coming too, you know." I pouted, but on the inside I was glad. This meant that I didn't have to be alone at all.

Amahté put his hand around my waist and began to lead me out of the room. We didn't get very far; my stomach growled. "Hmm. I guess we'll have to eat on the way."

We left the room, and the twins led me down the right-hand passage. I had never been down that way before; it was kind of depressing. All the walls were the same off-white, and there were hardly any skylights, like there were in the other hallway. Someone had made an attempt to brighten up the place; every thirty feet or so, there was a vase of flowers. But it didn't help much, because the vases were all the same, bland colors: dull purple, stained with gray.

At the very end of the hall was a plain doorway. Amahté opened it for me, and I stepped through into the most beautiful garden I had ever seen. It wasn't like any of the gardens in Egypt; I doubted that even the palace could compare to this.

There were so many trees, a rarity in Egypt. They were tall with wide, drooping leaves, providing shade for anyone who needed it. Some of them had flowers blooming among the leaves, red and orange and violet, and some bore fruit. I recognized some of the fruits, but some were like nothing I had ever seen before. On the ground, lining the pathways, the hedges were in bloom, filled with even more colors than the trees. There was fruit there, too.

"We can eat here," Amahté said, handing me some fruit. I accepted what he gave me, even though I didn't recognize some of it. I was confident that he wouldn't hand me anything unless he thought I would like it. And I did end up liking everything that he gave me, even if some of it was a little weird.

After we had finished (the twins finished much faster than I did; they had actually eaten breakfast), we headed out of the garden. I was led onto a path, winding through trees and wild bushes. That didn't last long, though. That path soon gave way to one that headed through a wild, untamed forest.

"Why does she live in all of this?" I gestured to the forest around me. "Why can't she just live in the main house? Wouldn't that be easier?"

Amahté shrugged. "Seer likes her privacy, so she lives at the very edge of the property. And there's no real need for her to move closer; people rarely come to see her."

"I see," I lied. The reason people rarely came to see her was probably *because* she lived so far from the main house, but I didn't point that out. Oh, well. It wasn't any of my business anyway, and I was willing to make the trek to her home. She was the one person who could hopefully give me answers.

We lapsed back into silence for a while. It made me uncomfortable seeing the brothers behaving so seriously, so

I tried to make conversation. "So, Akori," I mused, "are things going well with Amisi? I know you have an issue with the whole working thing."

He bit his lip. "Things are…fine."

"Is this about her working?"

"I am fine with the *idea* of her working, but not while I am around. Ab has been keeping me extra busy, trying his hardest to keep me away from her, and then when I do get to see her, she is working." He sighed. "I just wish that she would stop so we could spend time together."

I wasn't quite sure how to respond to that. I felt bad for Akori, because I knew where he was coming from; I didn't like it when Amahté tried to do research when he was with me. But Amisi had told me how she felt, and I thought I understood her, too. So I decided to try and compromise.

"Why don't you work with her?" I suggested. "At least until she gets used to the idea of not working. That way, she can work *and* you can spend time with her." I smirked, proud of my solution. I usually had trouble coming up with ways to solve problems like these.

"Perhaps," he said slowly. "Yes. That might work." He grinned at me. "Thank you, Fala."

I grinned back. "You're welcome." Then a patch of light through the trees caught my attention. "Akori, what's that? Are we supposed to be heading towards it?" Normally, I wouldn't have asked the second question, but I didn't want to wind up in the middle of something that would give me a tail. The wings were enough, thank you.

"That is where Seer lives, so that means yes, we are indeed supposed to be heading towards it."

Amahté was slightly ahead of us, so he reached the clearing first. When we broke through the trees, my first impression of the place was that it was way too dark. But then I remembered that Seer was blind, so I guess she didn't have any need for lighting. There was a small hut, made of sticks and held together with mud, in the center of the clearing. The roof was thatched over with leaves, and the whole thing looked like it defied reason by not falling down.

In front of the hut was an old woman crouched over a fire, chanting. That must have been the light I had seen.

The old woman was also sprinkling some sort of powder into the flames, which I assumed was responsible for the ridiculous amount of smoke in the air. Since she was also chanting some sort of incantation, and was the only woman in sight, I assumed that this was Seer.

"You assume correctly, child," Seer intoned, turning to face me. I was speechless; I hadn't said those things aloud, had I? "No, child. But your heart is screaming for the answers that I possess. It was difficult not to hear you."

"Alright…" I said sheepishly. The thought of having this strange woman in my head kind of frightened me, but the twins didn't seem to be fazed by it.

"Seer," Amahté began, "we were having some problems with the Osiris amulet, and we can't find the answers we need. So we were wondering—"

"If I would help you?" Seer finished for him. "Of

course I will, to the best of my ability. You two have always been such lovely boys; I am glad that you each found someone to suit your tastes." She turned to me. "Now, come here, my child. Fala, is it? Well, let me see what I can do for you."

In all honesty, it kind of freaked me out that the blind woman could tell where we all were. 'Not that that's a bad thing,' I thought quickly, in case she was still listening to my thoughts. I heard her chuckle quietly to herself, and I wondered if she was laughing at my thoughts or hers. I shuffled forward shyly, standing in the spot she indicated.

The old woman placed her wrinkled, brown hand on my forehead, and I stiffened. Her touch brought back something that I had nearly forgotten; something strange that had happened the very first night that I had known the demigods. It was the vision that I had seen of my Mwt and I…from my Mwt's point of view.

When the vision had finished, it was different from the first time. Before, I had just felt confused, because I didn't know what it meant. This time, however, I felt drained. I just wanted to sleep…

Sometime during the vision, I had ended up on the ground; Amahté was holding me, and Akori was standing right next to him, bent over me.

It was sort of odd, being held with wings. Amahté's arms were around me, but they weren't quite touching me; my wings were getting in the way. They were curled around my body, the way I had often seen a Mwt bird curl her wings around her chick.

I shook my head, trying to regain my composure. "What…How did I get on the ground?"

"You collapsed," Akori told me. "Amahté nearly died of shock when he saw you fall. If you do not mind my asking, what is that you were speaking of?"

"Talking about?" I repeated. "I was talking?"

"She will not remember it," Seer broke in. I jumped; I had thought that she was a little ways away, but she had come closer without my noticing. "You told them about your vision," she explained. "That was the first one you have ever had, correct?"

I nodded, and Amahté asked, "Yeah, you scared me when you just started to talk about the moon and Teanna and stuff. And then you just collapsed…" He shook himself, as if getting rid of some fear he had. "Was Teanna your Mwt?"

"Yes. Didn't I tell you that?"

"No, you didn't mention her name. But about this whole vision thing…when did you have it?"

"The very first night I met you two," I said. "You were both asleep, but I was wide awake. So I decided to take a walk, and that's when it happened." I turned to Seer. "But it's not like it happens all the time; that *was* my first one. So why did it happen at all?"

The woman frowned. "I cannot be sure. Some higher power has given you protection from beings such as myself; there is no way for me to tell what you are." My heart sank.

This strange woman had been my only way of getting answers. "However," she continued, "I can sense that these visions are the key to your past. Heed them."

"What past?" I said, annoyed. "I know all about my past! The present is what I need to know about, and the future. The past doesn't have to do with anything! I need to know why this is happening to me!"

"You do not even know your own Ab!" she snapped. "And as for why this is occurring, the answer to that is the amulet embedded in your body."

"But—"

"No, I cannot tell you why, child." Her voice was softer now, gentler. "A High God has visited me this day, just hours before you arrived. He has instructed me not to tell you of your origins, or of your connection with the Osiris amulet. I did question him as to why a High God would trouble himself; he merely said that it was a matter of safety." Amahté and Akori looked astonished; I guessed that the High Gods didn't come here often.

I, on the other hand, was furious. All I wanted, all I had *ever wanted* was to lead a normal life. I tried to do the best that I could with this strange turn my life had taken, but I didn't want to embrace this without my fair share of questions answered. Now even a High God was bent on keeping those answers from me.

"Do not be angry, Fala," Seer assured me. "Even with all his power, he did not wish to keep his mind or his heart from me. I would be able to answer your questions, if it were not for his order. But his heart was pure; he does not wish you any malice." She shook her head pityingly. "I was instructed to tell you that, when the time is right, your Ab will give you all the answers you desire."

This statement caught me off-guard. My Ab was alive? All these years, I had thought that he was dead, like my Mwt. I had *hoped* that he was dead, because if so, that meant he hadn't abandoned me. At worst I thought that my Mwt had never heard from him because he didn't know about me. He knew that I existed?

He knew that I existed, and he had left me to think that I was all alone in this world?

Abruptly, I was furious again. I had always stored away my anger towards my Ab, telling myself that he *must* have a good reason for leaving. That he *must* have a good reason for not coming to help me. Now I knew that that wasn't true, and the pent-up anger began to flow.

"My *Ab*?" I spat, standing up and pushing away from the twins. "You expect me to wait for *my Ab*?! I have spent *ten years* waiting for someone, *anyone* to come and help me, and he expects me to wait even longer?! I thought he was *dead*! I've never even met him, and I certainly don't want to now! I absolutely, utterly, and completely *hate him*!" With that, I turned and stalked off into the trees.

I knew it was childish. But I just couldn't forgive him for abandoning me and my Mwt. He knew about my Mwt in the first place, and if he knew about me, there was no reason for him not to help. What kind of person would *do* this—!

"Fala? Fala, wait!" Amahté called as he crashed through the forest. "Please don't be angry with Seer; if a High God gave her a direct order, she can't disobey it. Only another High God could allow her to go against those orders."

"That's not what I'm mad about," I spat. "My Ab left before I was even born. I don't even know his *name*. And now he just expects that we can be one big, happy family? Not a chance!"

Amahté shook his head. "That's not what she said, Fala. Seer said that your Ab would give you the answers you needed; that doesn't mean that he knows who you are right now. She got that bit of information from a High God."

"So?"

Akori came up behind Amahté, and answered my question. "Well, sometimes the High Gods can see things before they happen, and the things they see sometimes do not happen for a very long time. What she said does not mean that your Ab knows who you are; he might never know. It just means that he will answer your questions someday."

"I...I hadn't thought of it that way," I whispered. And for some reason, I started to cry, which was so embarrassing. I hardly ever cried. The last time I had even shed a tear was when my Mwt died. But I had been so stressed lately, and this had been my one hope. As ridiculous as it was, once the tears started flowing, I couldn't make them stop.

Amahté reached out and pulled me into a tight embrace. "Shh, it's okay, Fala, it's okay." Akori reached out and put a hand on my shoulder, trying to help Amahté comfort me. Which was completely stupid, because I shouldn't need comforting.

After a few minutes, I reluctantly pulled myself from Amahté's arms. "I'm sorry about that," I muttered. "It was stupid. I don't know why I started crying."

"I think I do," Akori said gently. "Fala, you are so stressed out, and under so much pressure, about things that you are not used to dealing with. It is alright if you need to let go every once in a while."

I just shrugged, wiping away the remnants of my tears, and turned to continue walking down the path. "I'm fine now, really. I've never cried like that, I don't know what got into me. But I should be fine n-AAHH!!!" The two looked up from the path, startled. I had tripped over a loose vine, and fallen into the ground, face-first.

I struggled to sit up. At first, I couldn't figure out why pushing myself up was so hard; then I realized that I was only using my right hand. I put a slight amount of pressure on my left wrist, and grimaced. Amahté came over to inspect my wrists and ankles.

"Clumsy little Fala," he chided. "It looks like you've sprained your left wrist, and your right ankle, too. What am I going to do with you?" As he talked, he was feeling my ankle, trying to see just how bad of a sprain it was. "It's not *too* bad," he said thoughtfully, "but you shouldn't walk on it until we can get it looked at and set."

"If I can't walk, how will we get home? And there is no

way you're carrying me. That would be just plain embarrassing." He had carried me before, but I definitely didn't want a repeat of *that* experience.

"So then we will not walk back," said Akori. He and Amahté were grinning like madmen at this point, and I started to worry about whatever plan they had in mind. I braced myself for whatever ridiculous suggestion that they were planning on proposing. "And if we cannot walk…" Akori began.

"Then we can *fly* back instead," Amahté finished, a triumphant grin on his face. "And this time, we can show you how to do it, too!"

"Oh, no!" I protested. "There is no way that you are going to get me to fly! I absolutely refuse!" The twins exchanged one quick glance, then grabbed me. Amahté put his arm around my waist, while Akori took a firm hold on my good arm. Together they pulled me up into the air with them, despite my protests.

"Fala, stop worrying," Akori soothed me. "You are going to be fine. We will not let anything happen to you."

"Yeah, right! Come on, you guys, I hate flying! You know that!" I squirmed around a little. Not too much, because I didn't want to fall, but enough to show that I was displeased.

"Fala, calm down and listen!" Amahté ordered. I obliged. "If you would just relax for a second, you would see that everything is fine. Is the altitude bothering you? The motion?"

I took a moment to consider what he was saying, and realized that he was right. Nothing was really bothering me; in fact, I was pretty comfortable.

"Well?" Amahté persisted. "Is anything bothering you?" I shook my head. "Exactly. What we were trying to tell you was that the whole being comfortable with flying thing comes with the wings. So you won't have any problem now." He shifted his grip on my waist ever so slightly. "Of course, if you ever felt like helping out, so we wouldn't have to carry all of your weight…"

I shook my head. "No. I can't; I don't know how!"

Amahté just shrugged. "Your loss…" he muttered.

Now that I was comfortable with flying, I took the time to study the forest below. From the sky, it looked almost like an intricate mosaic, full of browns and greens. I started trying to search for patterns in the foliage. I was so intent on what I was doing that I didn't notice Amahté steadily loosening his grip until he completely let go of me, and I was falling, falling towards the earth.

Chapter Six

What was he thinking?! He had dropped me! This was just like before—!

"Just a little while longer, Fala," Teanna assured her. "And then we can go home." The two were at the market by the Nile, gathering food for that evening's meal. Usually, the pair didn't come to this part of the river; the currents were strong here, and the young Mwt hated to see innocent children fall in and drown. But she had little money at the time, and the food was cheap here. And so she came, bringing her child with her.

Teanna turned to the merchant to give the woman her payment, but she was staring at the Nile in horror. Curious, Teanna turned, quickly realizing what the problem was.

"Fala!" she screamed. For, while she hadn't been looking, her child had fallen into the river. And she couldn't swim. Before she completely knew what she was doing, she was running to the river, jumping in to save her daughter. She was only four years old…

Teanna managed to pull her helpless child from the water. It was a miracle that they hadn't both been dragged under; the waters were especially unforgiving today. But her troubles weren't over yet; her child wasn't breathing.

She began to panic, trying frantically to pump air into her daughter's tiny body. She couldn't bear to lose her only child, her only real family. Yet it seemed that no matter how hard she worked, she couldn't get the girl to breathe. No one around her offered any assistance; they never did. Teanna usually tried to help a child if they were hurt, but no one offered the same helping hand to her.

Just as she began to give up hope, someone came by to try and help her. She couldn't see who the man was, as a hood covered his face. Still, she let him come nearer to Fala. There was nothing more that she could do; perhaps this man could help her daughter. As he pushed the hood back, Teanna gasped. This man was no stranger.

He placed one hand on Fala's chest, muttering as he did so. In the next instant, the girl was coughing, moaning, calling for her Mwt. Teanna pulled her little girl close, thanking any god that would hear her praise. She turned to the man next to her with tears in her eyes, grateful to him for saving her daughter's life. His daughter's life.

The man that was her husband.

'What was that?' I wondered. I shook my head quickly. Why had I had another vision? And at the worst possible time, too! I opened my mouth to yell for Amahté…but there was no need. Just as I opened my mouth, I felt a sharp tug on my back, keeping me from falling. 'Amahté,' I thought, covering my face with my hands.

"What is wrong with you, Amahté?" I questioned.

"Don't do that, ever again!"

"Okay, I won't," he answered. But his voice came from in front of me. I was sure that the pressure holding me up was coming from behind me. I peeked out from between my fingers. There was Amahté, hovering in front of me, a huge grin plastered to his face. I took my hands away from my face confused. Akori's laughter rang out behind me, so I figured that he must be the one holding me up.

I turned around to look at him (to glare, actually)...and almost felt my heart stop. *I* was holding myself up. Or, more accurately, my wings were. Akori *was* right behind me, but he wasn't touching me at all.

"I am only here to pull you up if you start to fall," he explained, "and Amahté is there to catch you. Just as a precaution, really. You are doing wonderfully, Fala."

I glared at each of the twins in turn. "When we get back," I threatened, "you two better hit the ground running. Because I am *so* going to kick both of you all the way from here to the pharaoh's palace."

"Well, then," teased Amahté, "maybe we should get a head start and leave now. You can find your way back on your own, right?"

My eyes widened. "No! Okay, okay, I won't! Don't leave me," I pleaded. If they left now, I'd be wandering the skies forever. Amahté laughed at my panicked expression, and tenderly took a hold of my left arm. Akori did the same with my right, and the two demigods guided me back to their home.

When we came to the garden, the twins gently and gracefully lowered themselves to the ground. I tried to follow their example, but I just ended up landing on my butt in between them. They laughed at me, of course.

Amahté helped me up, chuckling. "Come on," he said. "Let's get you to your room." I slung my arm around his shoulders so that I didn't have to put weight on my right leg; with his help, I managed to hobble to my room. Akori insisted that I should stay sitting on my bed until the family physician arrived, but I was antsy. I had never been one to just sit around, and that was what he wanted me to do. And so soon after I had resolved to work more, too!

The physician seemed to take forever to arrive. At first, I thought that the twins were playing a joke on me. The man was short, and seemed excessively clumsy. This was their physician? Were they kidding?

"Hello, Miss, um, Fala. What, uh, seems to be the, ah, problem?" I just pointed wordlessly at my ankle and my wrist; he came over to examine them. "Hmm…ah, yes, I see…uh-huh…" Maybe he *was* a physician. He certainly made enough annoying physician noises. "Well," he concluded, finally straightening up, "you seem to have, ah, sprained both your right ankle and your, ah, left wrist. Let's get that, um, set now, ah, shall we?" I nodded, biting my tongue to keep the flow of sarcasm to a minimum. After all, he was still a physician.

It took him all of ten minutes to get everything set and done, and then another five to lecture me on 'proper safety.'

151

I wanted to tell him that I didn't need a lecture; it was mostly common sense, like 'don't push yourself' or 'be careful on stairs'. Really I wasn't sure why we had needed the physician. He had just put two firm sticks on either side of my ankle and wrist and wrapped them with thicker bandages, then coated them in what smelled like resin. I could have done that.

Finally, after a few residual 'ah's and 'um's, he was gone. Amahté and Akori left shortly thereafter, saying that I needed my rest. Which I was extremely grateful for. Other than my little faint from meeting Khenti (which, I was told, only left me unconscious for about fifteen minutes), I hadn't had any sleep since before we left Egypt.

The day before, I had woken up early, worked the whole day (it was hard to find a place that would actually sell you food once you were branded a witch), and then come home. Amisi had taken me back here, we had run into Khenti, I had fainted and then woken up with wings (surprise!), and then gone to visit Seer. Of course, that was all in a day's work for me now!

I sighed. I must be half-delusional from sleep deprivation; either that, or living with demigods was really starting to get to me. I lay back on my bed, trying to relax, and pulled the tie out of my hair. It was getting really long; I hadn't cut it in almost a year. I'm not exactly sure why. In Egypt, long hair was beginning to come into style, and I guess I had thought that I'd try it. It was a good three inches below my waist. Amahté said he liked it long, but I was pretty sure that I should cut it soon.

I ran my fingers through my hair, trying to get out some of the tangles. Plus, if I focused on getting my hair untangled, I could avoid thinking about how stressful the past few days had been; that way I could completely relax. I had almost fallen asleep when I heard a knock at my door.

Miu pushed her way into my room almost as soon as I put my head on my pillow. "Fala?" she inquired, her voice strained. "May I speak with you for a few moments?" I pulled myself into a sitting position, being careful with my sprains.

"Yes, Miu?" I yawned.

"I am sorry, I know you are tired, but this is very important. I was wondering if you could perhaps tell me about your...visions?" I nodded, and proceeded to tell her everything that I could about them.

"Oh, yeah," I added sleepily, "I had another one today. I forgot to tell Amahté and Akori about it." I told her about my most recent vision. When I told her about the man I had seen, she stopped me.

"This man, do you know his name?"

I shook my head. "No; my Mwt didn't say his name, not even in the vision."

"Would you recognize him at all?"

"I don't know," I told her. "His face was sort of shadowed. I might know him if I saw him, but I can't be sure."

She sighed. "These...visions. Are you sure that they are real?"

"Yes," I answered. In fact, that was one of the few things that I *was* sure of. "I know they're real, because I remember them for myself. Like in the first one, I remember running alongside the Nile with my Mwt on that birthday. And I remember nearly drowning, and hearing my Mwt thank a man."

Miu nodded, but she was still frowning. "Alright, then. You should get some sleep now, and we can look into this some other time. Although I am not sure what we can do; I have never heard of this sort of thing happening." Of course not. No one ever knew what was going on with me. "On the positive side," she continued, "Amahté's cousins are in for the weekend."

I was lost. "What does that have to do with anything?" I wondered.

"Oh, I am sorry, I have forgotten to tell you. Tomorrow morning, Amahté has to assist me with a meeting. However, we did not want you to be alone, and the triplets— Amahté's cousins, that is—are your age. So I thought that you four could perhaps spend some time together." A play date. That's what she had done; she had set me up on a play date. I knew she was trying to be nice and help me out, but…

"Akori doesn't have anything tomorrow," I realized. "…Or is he busy, too?"

"Well…he has to help out as well, so…"

"Alright, then," I sighed. "But can I please get some sleep?" She nodded, seeming pleased that I had accepted her suggestion. I practically passed out as soon as she left, I was so tired.

I slept until almost noon the next day; the visit to Seer

had completely worn me out. Actually, I probably would have slept in even later if Amisi hadn't come to wake me up.

"Come on, Fala," she scolded, when I just rolled over and buried my face in a pillow. "You have to get up. The triplets are coming to visit you today; you must get ready."

Reluctantly, I sat up, trying to smooth back my mass of hair from my face. "Alright, I'm up, I'm up." I yawned. "Hey, weren't you supposed to try to cut back on work? Come on, we just had this conversation yesterday."

She shrugged. "Khenti chose someone to wake you. The servant that was called upon was a man. And he has a reputation for…well, for being a pervert. I did not think you'd want some stranger grabbing you…inappropriately first thing in the morning."

I blinked. "Oh…well…you're right." Then I frowned, and added, "If he had tried that, he probably would have ended up with a broken jaw." She giggled, and I rolled my eyes. "What? It would be his own fault."

She just shook her head. "Fala, you are the most outrageous person that I have ever known. I like it; it makes you unique."

"Well, that's one way of putting it. Some people would be a lot less generous."

"They do not know what they are talking about," she insisted.

We talked for a few more minutes, but then she had to leave so I could get ready. The outfits that Amisi had picked out for me had been put in the dresser, replacing the clothes

I could no longer wear. For meeting the triplets, I had a turquoise top, with small beads adorning the collar. The leggings were just black.

I had worried that I would have trouble moving around, because of my ankle, but there was no need. The setting kept my ankle firm enough that there was no evidence that I was injured, other than a slight limp. If that was all I had to deal with, then it was fine by me.

Glancing at the sundial, I saw that I still had about half an hour before the triplets showed up, so I decided to cut my hair. I found a small knife, similar to the one that I had used to cut my hair in Egypt.

When I had finished, my hair was just barely past my shoulder blades, just the length I liked it. I had just gotten everything cleaned up when there was a knock at the door.

"Come in!" I called, and the triplets entered.

"Are you Fala?" one of them demanded. The other two stood slightly behind her; one of them looked stand-offish, while the other just looked shy.

"Yeah, that's me," I answered. "And you are...?"

"Oops, sorry," the first girl said. "I'm Metit. This is Tameri—" she gestured to the stand-offish girl— "and the shy little one here is Chisisi. In case you haven't been able to tell, we're triplets." I laughed along with her at this.

Anyone could see that they were triplets. They all had russet brown hair of different lengths; Metit's came down to her chin, Tameri's came just past her shoulders, and Chisisi's went past her waist. Their skin was pale, and their eyes were a beautiful emerald green. Their ears were pointed, and they had pale pink fin-like wings on their backs and arms, so I assumed that they were water demigoddesses.

Since none of us wanted to stay in my room, we ended up walking around outside. It was a beautiful day out. I mostly talked to Metit; Chisisi was nice, but she was really quiet and shy. Tameri just tried to avoid talking to me altogether, and she never made eye contact with me. But Metit, Chisisi and I did talk about quite a lot.

"So you lived in Egypt?" Metit asked at one point.

"Yeah," I told her. "I actually lived there for most of my life. I haven't really been here for that long...honestly, it can't have been more than a few months."

"That is really neat," Chisisi said in that shy little way she had, peeking at me from behind her hair. She let it fall in front of her face, forming a kind of curtain between her and everyone else. "Is that how long you and Amahté have been together?"

"We've been together for about a month. But what about you two? Are you with anyone?"

Metit bit her lip. "...Sort of. Not really. You have to understand that most of us have an arranged marriage; your relationship with Amahté is sort of a rare thing. I mean, I have an *arranged* relationship..."

"Oh," I said slowly. "I'm sorry. I didn't—"

"It's fine," she interrupted. "You couldn't have known. Anyway, the guy that I'm promised to is really sweet, and we do get along. I could have ended up with someone awful, but

Ibenré and I have a pretty good relationship. Although not as good as Chisisi and Khai," she snickered.

Chisisi blushed. "S-So? Just because we happen to actually love each other does not mean that you can pick on us! And you should not pick on Khai when he is not here."

I decided to intervene on Chisisi's behalf. "I think it's great that you love him, Chisisi. You're so lucky." I didn't really know much about her situation, but I knew that if a girl actually fell in love with the man she was promised to, then she was extremely blessed. I knew girls that had hated their arranged husband so much that they had eloped to a foreign country.

This set off a whole new conversation about what the odds were of actually liking your betrothed. I was getting along really well with the two girls until Tameri decided to break into the conversation.

"Why does it matter?" she sneered. I winced; she had an unpleasant, nasally voice. "It is not up to you, anyway, and you don't even know anything about us! You still have your head filled with stupid human rules!" And with that, she turned and stomped away.

I stared after her, then turned and asked Metit, "What is she talking about?"

"...She agrees with a lot of the things our Aunt Kifi says. One of those things is that...well, she thinks you're no better than a stuck-up human."

I sighed. I guess being raised in the human world had its drawbacks when you were dealing with gods. But there wasn't much that I could do about that, now, was there? Everyone would just have to deal with me the way I was.

"Well," I said, trying to patch together our broken conversation, "I don't try to be stuck-up. If that's how I come off, then I'm sorry, but I'm not changing my personality just so the demigods like me." I shrugged. "I really don't care what other people think about me, especially if I don't know them."

Something that I said must have made Metit uncomfortable. "Yeah…Listen, I have to go. Maybe we can catch up some other time. See you around!" She stood and quickly hurried away.

Now, only Chisisi was left. "Are you leaving, too?" I asked her.

She shook her head. "No; I would like to stay. I do not always agree with my sisters. I care for them very much, but they sometimes discriminate too easily." I nodded in approval. Chisisi was the youngest, if only by a bit. Apparently she was also the most mature.

We spent a good chunk of the day together. When she finally had to leave, we promised to try to see each other again soon. I was glad that I had gotten along with at least one of the triplets.

Amahté and I had a late dinner together that night, out on my balcony. Once we had both finished, I left my chair to go curl up in his lap.

"How was your day with the triplets?" he asked.

"It was…interesting, to say the least. Tameri appears to hate me with a passion and Metit just kind of left. Chisisi and I got along really well, though."

He grinned. "Yeah, Tameri is a bit opinionated. Don't worry about Metit, though. She'll come around." I nodded, and he hugged me tightly.

"Isn't the moon beautiful?" Teanna mused. It shone down on the young couple, basking in the garden. Here they were safe from prying eyes; here they were free to be with one another.

"It is beautiful," her lover admitted. "But not as lovely as you." She blushed, burying her face in his chest. He had a talent for bringing a blush to her cheeks.

Still, she couldn't keep her eyes away from her new husband for long; she was too much in love. Pulling her face back so she could see him, Teanna smiled timidly up at him. He smiled back, glad that she was happy. The two loved each other more than anything. As they sat together beneath the moon, they felt that the world couldn't be more right.

I blinked, and was back in the present. Amahté was looking at me, confused; unfortunately, I was just as lost.

I took a deep breath, and said, "I think we should go see your Mwt." Amahté immediately understood that this was important, so he helped me up without hesitation.

We found Miu in her usual spot: the library. She had been here almost every day since I had arrived. I felt bad about eating up her schedule, and I had told her that she didn't have to do this, but she insisted that she wanted to. Honestly, I thought that she just wanted to figure out what was going on before anything else unexpected happened.

"Hello Fala, Amahté. How are you?" She frowned then, noticing our tense expressions. "Is something wrong?" Reluctantly, I told her about my most recent vision. "It happened again?" she exclaimed.

"Yes," I replied tiredly. "And it keeps getting clearer." I couldn't get through one day without something strange happening, could I? Miu seemed to be following the same train of thought, and she sighed.

"It is getting late," she said. "We cannot do anything about it now. Go get some rest, and we will deal with it the day after tomorrow." When I gave her a confused look, she explained, "The meeting today ran over; it will continue tomorrow."

"Oh, alright. I'll find Amisi and we can do something."

"Actually…" Amahté said hesitantly, "Mwt has arranged for you to spend the day somewhere tomorrow. Amisi will be helping Akori. We don't want to leave you alone, so…you will be staying with Ab." He hung his head guiltily.

"Khenti?" I asked, incredulous. Amahté nodded, biting his lip. "He hates me!" But no matter what I tried, no matter what I said, the fact remained. I would have to spend a day with Khenti.

~*~

When I woke the next morning, Ra was shining brightly. It wasn't too hot or too cold outside, and there was a beautiful breeze. I could hear birds chirping outside my bedroom window.

But none of that made me feel any better, because I would be spending the day with Khenti. Who would, quite possibly, lock me in the dungeon. If there was a dungeon in this place; I was sure he'd come up with something just as bad. Maybe I should have an escape plan ready…?

I dressed slowly, not wanting to deal with Khenti anytime soon. I was trying to avoid the confrontation for as long as possible; I didn't want to fight this early in the morning. Hopefully I wouldn't have to fight at all—I didn't like Khenti, sure, but I didn't want to let Amahté down. A fight from me would only cause more problems for him and Akori.

After I had dressed, I sat down to wait. Amahté had said that Khenti would come and find me, but he couldn't be looking forward to this anymore than I was. Maybe he would mysteriously forget that he had to get me…

My hopes were crushed as the door opened, and Khenti walked into the room. He looked just as angry as I felt. Without saying a word, he threw one glance in my direction and stalked away. Assuming that I was supposed to follow, I got up and walked after him, glaring at his back the whole way. I didn't want to cause trouble for the twins, but I certainly wasn't going to give Khenti a license to do whatever he wanted to me.

We walked through the maze of hallways in silence. That was fine by me; I didn't have anything to say to him. At least, nothing that was considered appropriate.

Khenti led me further into the estate than I had ever been before. The further we walked, the less people we saw. The wilting flowers in their drab vases vanished; no one had tried to make this part of the estate look any better. I wondered idly if Khenti had anything to do with that; I knew that Miu was the one behind most of the efforts elsewhere.

After a while, the vases were completely replaced with portraits of frowning men staring down at us. That did absolutely nothing for my mood.

Eventually, we came to a decorative wooden door. Once again, it seemed to me that demigods had no sense of practicality. There was no reason for a door to be decorated with an extensive battle scene. I was pondering this when Khenti unlocked the door and said shortly, "My office. Don't touch anything; just sit over there." That made the door make sense; I could see someone as twisted as Khenti wanting a battle scene on his door.

Since he had decided to give an order without throwing in an insult, I decided to return the favor by listening...for the moment. I sat down in a corner of the small room; I wanted to stay as far away from Khenti as possible.

There was already someone else there. Khenti went right over and started talking to him, so I assumed that they had some business together. Why could I see this business and not whatever Amahté was involved in?

While those two talked, I took the opportunity to look around the room. Unlike the door outside, there was hardly any decoration in this room. In terms of furniture, there were only a few chairs, a desk and a bookshelf; that was all. It seemed to be enough, though.

Khenti suddenly stood and left the room, leaving both me and the stranger behind. The other man turned to me, looking as if he were studying a painting. I didn't pay him much attention. Everyone else looked at me that way already; they couldn't seem to accept my views. Why should one more demigod make any difference? He was just going to look.

Or at least that was what I thought. Before long, he asked, "You, there. Girl. What is your name?" I resisted the urge to roll my eyes. Did he think that I didn't know who he was talking to? I was the only other person in the room.

"My name is Fala," I told him. "What is *your* name?" I thought that was a fair question to ask. If he was planning on interrogating me, then I at least deserved to know his name.

"You may call me Lord Anhuri," he announced, as though I was so privileged to call him that. "Khenti has requested that I do a bit of…investigative work. None of the dirty bits, of course. But I do so enjoy the questioning." He leaned towards me, now completely absorbed in what he was doing. "Now, tell me…who were your parents? Where are they?"

I was caught off guard. Why did he care? "That is none of your business," I said as firmly as I could. I didn't want him digging through my life; I didn't even really know who he was.

"Oh, but it is. Is there something you have to hide, little Fala?"

"No. I just don't like someone that I don't know asking me random questions."

He frowned, and for the first time, his composure slipped. "You have no right to withhold information from me, girl." Then he sighed, and his voice grew sweet again—sickly sweet, like poisonous honey. "And besides, I am already aware that your Mwt is dead, and that she has been for a long time."

I clenched my teeth. "It's none of your business," I spat again. "Leave my Mwt out of this!"

"Touchy subject, I see. I wonder why...." he mused. "You know, the interesting thing about you is that I couldn't find any information about your Ab." Why had he been looking in the first place? His face grew contorted with fiendish glee. "Are you a bastard child? A child to a worthless Mwt, unwanted by her Ab?"

"My parents loved each other very much! My Ab...my Ab died just before I was born!" Of course, I was lying now; I had just learned that he was alive. But I couldn't stand hearing him talk about my Mwt like that! Plus, even if I was angry with my Ab (whoever he was), I wasn't one to let people be insulted behind their back. Unless Khenti was the one being insulted, but that was a different story.

My lie pushed Anhuri over the edge. His composure completely left him, and the venom in his voice was no longer hidden. "Listen, you foolish girl," he threatened, "I will find something about you. I am not about to let a *thing* like you defile the name of the demigods!" Without another word, he turned and left the room.

I shook my head in disgust. I could not see how anyone could find such joy in defiling others. How would he like it if I went through his past? Even worse than that was the thought that he wasn't the only one with such a twisted sense of humor; I could name plenty of humans that shared in that particular kind of desire.

Khenti walked back into the room shortly after Anhuri left, and he was clearly disappointed. My guess was that Khenti had hired the demi-god to try and get rid of me. As he walked past me, his muttered curses only served to strengthen my suspicions.

I knew it was wrong, but I couldn't help teasing him just a bit. "Was that your business associate?" I asked calmly. "He wasn't very good at his job, was he?"

The corner of Khenti's mouth twitched downwards. "Quiet, girl. You are annoying me."

My eyes narrowed. "I really don't care. I can do whatever I want when *you* go out of your way to have me interrogated."

His head shot up, and his nostrils flared. If looks could kill, then I would be dead many times over. "You can do no such thing! You are nothing but the daughter of a whore!"

Before I knew quite what I was doing, I had punched Khenti square in the face. I heard a satisfying crunch as his nose broke, and then I was running out the door; I didn't expect him to just lie there.

And I was right. I heard him yell, "Get back here, you

infidel!" Then he was running after me. I knew that he would catch me. My ankle was still healing, and my sprint had already turned into more of a limp. I risked a glance over my shoulder; sure enough, Khenti was gaining on me, and I had never seen him look so angry. Oh Ra, this was *not* how I wanted to die…

I skidded around a corner, praying that it was an escape route; I had no idea where I was going.

Well, it wasn't an escape route, but there was a wide open door that would work. I dashed into the room, not bothering to see what room it was, and slammed the door shut behind me. Luckily, there was a bolt on the door; I quickly slid it into place, hoping that Khenti didn't have some way of getting through.

For a few long moments I held my breath, but Khenti's angry cries soon assured me that he couldn't get through. I sank to the floor, massaging my strained ankle. I hoped that this didn't mess up my recovery.

~*~

"So, how was your day with Ab?" Amahté asked. The two of us, as well as Miu, were sitting in the garden, eating dinner. I hadn't had to wait long for Khenti to leave; patience obviously wasn't his strong point. It had taken me longer to find my way back to my room than it had taken for him to go.

"It was…boring. Nothing interesting happened," I lied. I knew that Amahté usually didn't agree with his Ab, but with

Miu sitting right there, I wasn't sure what to say.

"Really?" he inquired, smirking.

"Really."

He shook his head. "How is your fist? Most anyone would hurt themselves punching a demigod."

I shrugged. "It wasn't like I didn't have a reason. He brought it upon himself."

"What did he do?" It was an innocent question, but it made me angry all over again. "Fala?"

"He called my Mwt a whore," I answered through gritted teeth.

"He what? Fala, are you sure—"

"Yes, I am sure that is what he meant! He said it flat out. He has no right to say that about her, especially with her being in the afterlife! I wasn't about to let him—" I broke off. I was rambling, and I was angry; if I didn't stop myself now, I would say something that I would regret later. I closed my eyes, trying to calm down.

"Fala?"

"Yes, Amahté?" I didn't open my eyes. I was still trying to be calm.

Amahté touched my arm, and I opened my eyes. "Fala, you're right. He had no right to say something like that." He pulled me into a tight embrace. "But next time, please just walk away. I don't want him to have an excuse to throw you out."

I nodded, finally relaxed enough to think rationally. "I will try. I don't know how well that will go, but..."

He silenced me with a quick kiss. "All I'm asking you to do is try."

"Ah-hem!" Both Amahté and I jumped. Akori had come up next to us, completely unnoticed. I blushed, and tried to pull myself from Amahté's embrace, but he just held me tighter.

"Hello, Akori. Is there something you need?"

"I am sorry for the interruption, but I thought it would be best to spare our Mwt." I looked over to where Miu was sitting; I had completely forgotten about her. She had been silent the whole time. "And," Akori continued, "I did need to tell you something. Aunt Kiwu and Uncle Itennu want to meet with you, Fala."

I grimaced. "Can I say no?"

He laughed. "No, I am sorry. They are actually already expecting you. But do not worry, they will not bite." I sighed, standing up. It seemed like *everyone* wanted to meet the strange little…what exactly was I? I definitely wasn't human, but there was no way I could be a demigoddess. Maybe a…demi-demigoddess? I really didn't know. Maybe I should have paid more attention when my Mwt had tried to teach me these things.

As I walked back to my room, I couldn't help thinking about all of this. I thought about asking Amahté what I was, but I was pretty sure that he and Akori had no more ideas than I did.

When I got back to my room, I was surprised to find that the door was already partially open; I always closed it behind me.

"Hello?" I called, pushing the door open all the way. "Who's here?"

A figure shot up on the other side of my bed. "S-Sorry, I just...Miss Miu told me to...Fala? Is that you?" the girl gasped.

"Yes, it's me," I said, trying to figure out who this girl was.

"Oh, it has been so long! Well, I suppose it really has not been that long, but still—I have not seen you since I lived in our home village!" What was she talking about? I hadn't had any friends in my village, people would hardly speak to me. I had been getting ready to move.

There wasn't anyone I thought this could be. Except for maybe...Kemreit! That's who this girl was. She had gone missing, and I had put my plans on hold to try and find her. Now, I suppose, I knew where she had gone.

"How did you get here, Kemreit? Why did you leave?" Now that I recognized her, I had so many questions. We hadn't been very close before she had gone, but I could always count on her, and she was always so nice. I was lucky that she had recognized me; she had changed so much. Her hair was now dark brown instead of dirty blonde, and some of her work tan had faded.

"Well, you were moving away, and I did not want to be left in that town; and the only reason I did not get fired was because of you."

"Oh, no that's not true," I laughed, but it probably

was. She tried hard, but Kemreit was more than a little clumsy; more often than not, she had needed my help.

"Yes, well, I...oh, you are going to laugh at me, I know it, but I just prayed to Ra that I would have somewhere to go. Next thing I knew, Missus Miu was offering me a job and a place to stay here."

"Kemreit," I scolded, "I told you that you could have come with me. You didn't have to stay on your own." I had actually wanted her to come—it would have been nice to know someone in my new home.

"Yeah..." I immediately felt bad for making it sound like it was her fault. I hadn't meant to; it was mostly mine. Her whole family, everything she had ever known, had been in our home town. The only difference between us was that she had no desire to move to a better place; I did.

I went over to her and put my hand on her shoulder. "I'm glad you found a place here," I told her. "Have they been treating you kindly?" If Khenti had been a jerk to her, then he was going to pay.

"No one really pays attention to me. I think I prefer it that way; I do not want to have to deal with Master Khenti on a bad day." She laughed timidly. "I am happy here. The other servants—the ones that notice me, anyway—are really nice. What about you? How in the name of Horus did you get here?"

I bit my lip. Kemreit had never been one who could deal with unusual situations. I wasn't sure how to tell her about the strange turn my life had taken. I decided to get it all over with at once. "It's a long story," I began, "but basically, I accidentally inherited a divine item—" she wouldn't know about the Osiris amulet— "and for some reason, that made me grow wings." I flinched at the word. "Oh, and do you know Amahté? Khenti's son?" She nodded weakly. "He is courting me."

Kemreit sank onto my bed, shocked. I didn't blame her; I was still having a hard time dealing with all of this, and it was *my* life.

After a moment, Kemreit said, "...Fala...Master Amahté sent me to help you...he wanted me to pick out a dress for you." She laughed weakly. "With your fashion sense, I am not surprised that you need help." I smiled back at her. I was sure that it wasn't easy to have a normal conversation with me. "Now, then," she muttered, "what should you wear?"

She wandered over to my wardrobe, scrutinizing its contents. Finally, a triumphant grin spread over her face, and she pulled out...another gown. Eew. I made a face; I was so sick of all the gowns. Did *everyone* around here have to dress as if they were from the palace? "Kemreit," I begged, "please, isn't there anything else I can wear? What's wrong with what I have on?"

Kemreit just rolled her eyes and handed me the gown. As she did, her eyes strayed to my wings. She couldn't seem to look away. I was wondering why...until I remembered that Kemreit loved heights. Her Mwt used to take her up to the tops of cliffs (apparently, that was more of an honor to the

172

gods than just praying at home). Even after her Mwt's death, Kemreit had often gone up there just for the view. She had once told me that if she had one wish, it would be to have wings.

Why did I have to know that?

"Come on," I sighed. "I still have plenty of time before lunch." She looked confused. "I'm going to take you flying." Kemreit had always been there for me, no matter what kind of situation I was in. I owed her something.

I pulled her gently to the balcony; she was staring at me, wide-eyed, like a child who was being promised a new toy. I picked Kemreit up in my arms (good thing she was one of the tiniest people I had ever met), and stood on the wide, stone railing.

'Please let me be able to do this,' I prayed. Then I jumped.

At first I was falling. I couldn't get my wings to work properly, and for a wild moment, I thought we were going to crash. Then, thank the gods, I felt a familiar pressure at my back, and we were flying.

It was so easy! It was like I had been flying for my whole life, though I had only done it once before. Kemreit was laughing, the wind whipping her short hair around her small face.

Being the show-off that I was, I couldn't just settle for gliding. I did a series of loops, leaving Kemreit giggling in delight. I was actually enjoying this just as much as she was; maybe it came with the wings.

Finally, though, I had to land. I reluctantly headed back to my balcony; now that I was enjoying flying, I didn't want to stop. But I had to sometime. I landed (on my feet this time), and set Kemreit down.

"That was amazing!" she exclaimed. I was impressed myself, though not with the flying. I hadn't thought that I could land that gracefully. Take that, Amahté!

"I'm glad you liked it," I told her, smiling.

She grinned back. I had always loved her youthfulness; she was so perky and full of energy all the time. "Thank you very much, Fala." Then she made a face. "But that does not mean that I can get you out of this lunch meeting."

I groaned. Of course. I reluctantly accepted the offered gown and went to change.

"Do not worry," Kemreit assured me when I was done. "I am sure that you will be fine. It is just lunch; you are not going off to battle."

I rolled my eyes. That was easy for her to say. Although, considering how badly my first meeting with Khenti had been, things couldn't go any worse.

At least, I hoped not.

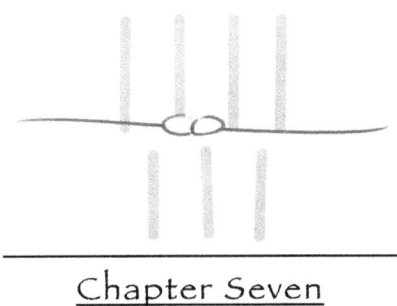

Chapter Seven

"So, Fala my dear, what are your interests?" Kiwu asked. She was a heavy-set woman with a booming voice, and she definitely liked to hear herself talk. It was impossible to ignore her. She wore a lot of ruffled clothing, so I couldn't be sure what was different about her, but if she moved the right way, I thought I could see scales.

Her husband Itennu, on the other hand, was just the opposite. He was a small, quiet man. Oddly enough, his appearance reminded me of a vulture, while his personality was more like that of a kitten. I couldn't help but wonder at the odd combination.

Things were actually going pretty well. At least, nothing had been broken or horribly mangled. I was still feeling just as awkward as I always did around the twins' family. So far, though, there had only been safe topics. I wasn't sure if that was because she was being kind, or if Miu had warned her about which topics to stay away from.

I wasn't sure how to answer Kiwu's question. My interests were simple ones; music, spending time with friends, and sometimes I liked to cook. I wasn't sure what 'acceptable' hobbies were around here, and I didn't want to make a bad first impression.

"Do you like music?" Kiwu prompted.

"...Yes," I told her. At least that was something, however small.

"Wonderful!" she boomed. How could anyone be so loud? It just didn't seem natural—it *couldn't* be natural! "Have you ever tried embroidery?" she continued. I shook my head. "No? Then you shall have to try it soon, my dear! It frees the soul!"

I had to struggle not to laugh. Free my soul? What in the name of Isis was she talking about? Besides, it probably wasn't a good idea to put any sort of sharp object in my hands. I was clumsy enough that it probably wouldn't end well.

Itennu leaned over and whispered something in her ear. The woman looked comical in her surprise.

"Well, I am terribly sorry, my dear, but it seems that Itennu and I really must be going. I look forward to our future luncheons!"

"Future? Wait, what do you—"

"Tomorrow's lunch promises to be especially delicious! We shall see you then!"

"Wait, I still don't know..."

But they were already out the door. Was it too much to ask for these people to wait around long enough to actually *talk* to me? Where was the fire?

I heard someone snicker, and I looked up, only to see

Amahté standing in the doorway. "You just had the most ridiculous look on your face," he told me.

I shook my head. "What do you expect? I think that was the longest—and loudest—lunch of my entire life."

"Don't worry, you'll get used to Aunt Kiwu after a while. She's not so bad; she's just *loud*."

"I figured that out on my own, thanks," I said sarcastically. "But what did she mean about 'future luncheons' exactly?"

Amahté looked uncomfortable. "Well… it's just that… considering everything that's been happening around you lately…"

"Amahté, if you're going to say something, then say it. Don't stand there sputtering like a moron."

He still hesitated, but this time I got an answer out of him. Too bad it wasn't a good one. "We wanted to make sure that you weren't alone, just in case anything else… weird happened."

I glared at him. "You're keeping me under *surveillance?* Is that what's going on?" He nodded. "Well that's just fantastic, Amahté. Great job keeping me informed."

"Well, I just told you, didn't I?" he joked, smiling crookedly. I walked by him without responding; there was no way I was going to let him off *that* easily. "Fala? Fala, come on!"

"—sure we could work something out," someone was saying. "Please, allow me to come up with an acceptable solution." Was that… Khenti? Khenti was being polite? I hadn't known that was even possible.

Of course, I couldn't let this momentous discovery go unchecked. I just *had* to know who he was being so nice to. So I rounded the corner at break-neck speed—

Only to be dragged back by a panicked Amahté.

"What are you doing?" he hissed.

I just shrugged. "I'm going to investigate; your Ab is actually being nice. What's wrong with that?"

"What's wrong," he told me, "is that he is talking to *Lord Osiris!* You know, the god of the dead? One of the thirteen most powerful gods to ever exist?"

Osiris was *here?* Why in the name of the pharaoh would he be here?

I wondered for a moment, and then I realized that it didn't matter. His stupid amulet had completely messed up my life; now I was going to make him fix it.

I marched right up to him, ignoring Khenti's sputtered protests and Amahté's whispered warnings. "Why are you here? What do you want?" I demanded.

"Fala, you can't talk to a High God that way!" Amahté insisted.

"Oh yes I can!" I countered. "He's already ruined my life, there's not much else that he can take from me."

"That is a bit harsh, is it not?" Osiris said. "You are happy with this young man, are you not?"

"*That* is none of your business," I told him. "But if you must know, I don't think that he makes up for losing my job, my home, my Mwt's belongings—" He flinched when I mentioned my Mwt. Well, if he couldn't live with ditching his wife and child then he shouldn't have done it! "—and I was run out of my town, and now I don't even know what I am! It's your amulet's fault that this all happened, so hurry up and fix it!!"

He sighed, and in that moment I thought that I had seen him before. But that was ridiculous; it was probably just his likeness that I recognized. It was everywhere, after all.

"I am truly sorry that all of this has happened to you," he said softly. "I cannot do anything about your town, but if you would like, I can find you a home somewhere else."

"It isn't just that," I protested.

"Please, Lord Osiris, she doesn't know what she's talking about," Khenti whimpered, pushing in front of me. "She isn't anything important, you needn't listen to her—"

"Khenti, shut up!" I snarled, pushing him away. "Look, Osiris. I'm sure that you didn't intend for this to happen when you gave your wife the amulet, but I shouldn't have to suffer for it. Why don't you just fix everything by making me human again?"

"I cannot do that."

"What? You're a High God, why can't you—"

"I can never make you human," he interrupted, "because you never were a human. Even my power cannot make you what you never were; it is impossible."

I didn't have a response. I had never been human? How was that possible? My Mwt had been beautiful, but overall she had just been an average woman. I was positive that she was human. So that meant…

"Let me guess," I mumbled, "my Ab is the one who isn't human. Everything just comes back to him, doesn't it? Ugh, why couldn't my Mwt marry someone normal?"

"I am quite certain that your Ab cares for you," Osiris insisted. "He must have had a reason for leaving—"

"You're one to talk; you abandoned your family, too."

"Fala—"

"I did not abandon them!" he thundered, and for the first time in his presence, I was afraid. "I did it to protect them," he continued more quietly.

I didn't answer. It wasn't right to argue with any sort of god; I should have learned that by now. Besides, I may not have been an overly religious person, but I still wanted to get into the afterlife, so arguing with the Lord of the Dead probably wasn't the best idea.

Amahté put his arms around me. "Come on, Fala," he said softly, "we can figure this out. Let's go, you don't need to be upset anymore."

"I'm not upset…"

Osiris sighed. "One such as you should not lie. Would you like my help or not?"

"But you said—"

"I said that I could not make you human, and that is true. However, I do have the ability to take back the amulet, which would allow you to revert to human form." He paused for a moment, glancing at Khenti. "It would have to be done at my estate, though."

I looked up at Amahté, wondering if he would be alright with my leaving. He just nodded, and smiled kindly at me. Ah, well. At this point, what did I have to lose? "…Fine. I will leave with you tomorrow."

I didn't wait for him to respond; I just turned and walked away, pulling Amahté with me.

"You shouldn't have argued with him," Amahté said as soon as we were out of hearing range. "I could have helped you…"

"No, you couldn't have," I sighed. "He's the only one who can even attempt to fix this mess."

"…Alright."

We walked in silence for a few minutes, not really having a destination, before Amahté said, "Fala? I… I'm sorry I dragged you into this."

I just shrugged. "It's fine. I… I didn't mean what I said about you back there; I was just trying to make a point. There are other good things that have happened, too. I just… I want to be able to go home after all this is over. There's no way that I could put up with Khenti for the rest of my life."

He laughed. "That's alright; I can completely understand the feeling. Maybe we could move to Egypt… together?"

Oh, great. I didn't need Amahté getting all mushy and romantic on me *now*. That would just complicate things. So I didn't answer him, and I shamelessly ducked into the closest room (which thankfully was my room), muttering, "I'll think about it."

I shut the door behind me and collapsed onto my bed. This was just too much for one girl to deal with! I had no idea what I was supposed to do after my visit with Osiris. Should I stay here, with Amahté? I wanted to return to Egypt, but if I wasn't human, then I wasn't sure if I could.

I sighed. There wasn't anything that I could do right now but wait. Why hadn't I gone with Osiris right away?

The day passed slowly. Everyone was busy with their daily duties, and Khenti didn't trust me enough to let me help the twins. I probably wouldn't be able to do much, but I would still be there. And anything would be better than just sitting here, wondering what would happen when Osiris made me normal—or at least, as normal as I could be.

When I had exhausted my limited list of things to do, I dug through my drawers until I found the vial of sleeping draught that Amahté had left for me. I downed it all in one gulp; if it knocked me out for a few extra hours, it wasn't a problem.

It didn't take long before my dreams overtook me.

Lost in the halls, Teanna called for her husband. She had been looking for him all morning, but he was nowhere to be found. And the servants wouldn't answer her; she had the sneaking suspicion that they had been ordered to keep quiet.

She had thought that he would be excited over their future child. Instead, he had become distant, withdrawn.

After wandering around for what seemed like hours,

she stumbled across his office. Teanna pushed the door open as quietly as she could, hoping that her husband would be inside.

When she glanced inside, she found him sitting at his desk. He looked up and smiled, but she still hesitated.

"Why?" she asked softly. He understood what she was asking.

"I cannot stay in Egypt with you, not anymore. You would be miserable if you stayed here, but in Egypt I cannot help to raise the child."

She blinked back her tears. "But that means—!" She could not go on.

He smiled gently. "Yes. We can be together no longer. Ironic, is it not? We overcome every obstacle only to be separated now."

She shook her head. "It isn't fair! Why do you have to stay here? Isn't there some way, some loophole that will allow you to come with me?"

"No, love." Teanna sobbed harder, and he pulled her into his embrace. "I will come see you when I can, I swear it. But… perhaps it is better this way. You and the child will be safer this way."

"I can't take care of a baby on my own…"

"You don't give yourself enough credit, dearest. And I will watch over the girl as best I can." He pushed her away just enough so that he could look into her eyes. "It is going to be a girl, you know."

"…What do you want to name her?"

"I don't really mind what she is called. She is going to be healthy, and that is all that matters. You can name her."

"No!" she cried. "No, please, I want you to name her. If you choose our baby's name, then I will always have something to remember you by... she will always have something from you. Please, just give me this."

Her husband sighed, running his fingers through her hair. "I don't want that to be the only thing you have from me." He reached into his pocket and pulled out a small necklace. "Here, take this."

She looked at the trinket in her hand. "...An amulet?"

"This is a special amulet. It will protect you, and when the time comes, it will protect our daughter."

Teanna closed her fingers around the amulet, holding it close to her as if she could force herself to wake from this nightmare if she squeezed tightly enough.

He kissed her forehead lightly. "Why don't we call our girl... Fala. That is a lovely name, don't you think?"

She tried to smile, to respond, but she couldn't speak around her tears.

He pulled her close once more, gave her his shoulder to cry on. When at last her tears ran dry, she pulled back to look at him.

"I love you, Teanna," he said. He spoke softly, as if his words were a physical blow.

She took the words as comfort. "I love you too, Osiris. So, so much."

I sat up, gasping. My Mwt's pain had been so vivid... I

had to tell Amahté.

I looked around, hoping that someone would be there, but no one was. In fact, this didn't even look like my room! It was bigger and much more… girly. Almost disgustingly so. Where in the name of Ra was I?

"Do you like the room?" a voice asked from the door. I jumped and turned to see who it was, though a part of me already knew.

It was him. The man who had abandoned my Mwt years ago, who had been mortified by my birth. Osiris. My Ab.

For a few minutes we stood there, silent. I didn't want to offend him—I still wanted him to fix me—but there was no way in the pharaoh's name that I was going to be nice to him. Not after all the trouble he had caused me. I was glad to have some answers after all this time, but I was angry with him for letting my Mwt die the way she did. Wasn't the amulet's purpose to protect her?

He never stopped smiling at me, but I could tell that he was just as nervous as I was.

Finally, I came up with a question that I hoped would not betray my emotions.

"Why are you here?" My voice shook.

"This is where I live," he told me. "I did not want to leave you in that demigod's home for much longer; he treats you so poorly. You were asleep when I came to get you."

"So you just kidnapped me?"

He frowned. "I did no such thing. I am only trying to

look out for you, Fala."

"Maybe you should have looked out for my Mwt like you promised!" I hissed.

"I did everything I could to protect her," he protested. "The amulet should have protected her; that murderer was not supposed to be a danger."

"'Should have' doesn't cut it! My Mwt is dead because of you!"

He turned away, silent. I knew I was being hurtful, but I couldn't bring myself to forgive him. Osiris had sworn to take care of my Mwt whether he was with her or not, and when that failed he didn't even try to help me. I wasn't going to let him make us a family just because he felt like it.

"Would you like to see her?" he said softly.

I was caught off guard. "See who?"

"Your Mwt. Would you like to see her?" he repeated.

"But—my Mwt is dead, I can't..."

Osiris smirked. "Of course you can. She lives on my property now; I may bring to her whomever I wish." Riiight. The whole Lord of the Dead thing.

I just nodded, unable to speak. I wanted to see her again so badly, but I was afraid. What would she think of me? Would she even want to talk to me, surrounded by paradise?

What if she was disappointed in me? That was my greatest fear. I had worked so hard, trying to do only what I thought would make her proud. But what if I had been wrong?

Osiris gently took my arm, and all of a sudden we were

flying through darkness. "It will take a minute to arrive," he said calmly, as if this was the most natural thing in the world. "This is for the souls who have yet to be judged."

I shivered and moved closer to him. This was one of the last places I wanted to get lost.

Then, just as abruptly as our journey had started, it stopped.

I almost burst into tears. We were no longer surrounded by darkness. There was a brook nearby, providing the only sound to the otherwise silent place.

And sitting right in the middle of it was a perfect replica of the house I had shared with my Mwt.

"Oh, Osiris, is that you?" Her voice sounded so sweet and caring, just like I remembered it. But I was so afraid to turn and face her. "I didn't think you were coming back so— Fala? Fala, baby, is that you?"

The next thing I knew, my Mwt had thrown her arms around me, crying, "Oh, it is you! My beautiful baby girl's all grown up! Oh, Fala, sweetie, I missed you so much."

She loosened her grip, and I took the chance to turn and face her. My Mwt looked just like I remembered her; thick, curly brown hair and big brown eyes. She was shorter than me now, but not by much.

"I… I missed you too, Mut."

She smiled brightly at me, before gasping, "Wait! This doesn't mean you're dead, does it? You're too young, baby girl! Osiris, send her back, Fala doesn't belong here yet."

"Mut, calm down," I laughed, putting my hands on her

shoulders. "I'm not dead. I just... *he* said that I could see you." I shot a glance in his direction, though I was sure that she knew who I was talking about.

"Oh, well, okay then. If you're sure that you are okay..." She bit her lip; she was probably trying to decide if she should believe me or if I was in denial.

"She is not dead, Teanna," Osiris said softly. "You can stop worrying."

My Mwt smiled at him, and in that single smile I could see all the love and devotion she held for him. It made me feel bad that I had been such a jerk, but how could I know?

"So, Mut..." I struggled to come up with something to say. "Is this... all of it? It would kind of depress me, the living alone all the time."

"Hmm? Oh, no, dear, this is just my special place. I come here when I want to see your Ab." I flinched, but she had looked towards Osiris, so she didn't notice. "Would you like to meet your grandmother?"

She started to pull me away, but I stopped her. "No... no, Mut, I just wanted to see you." My voice broke on the last word.

She frowned, concern evident in her eyes. "Fala, what's wrong? Are you okay?"

I took a deep breath to compose myself. It wouldn't do to upset her when we had only just met up again. "I'm fine, Mut. I just really missed you. Things have been so crazy lately."

She cocked her head to the side. "Really? Oh, is that

what the wings are from?" I flinched, and she reached up to ruffle my hair. "I think they're beautiful, Fala."

"Of course, Mut," I muttered. She could have them, if she wanted. I sure didn't.

"You look stressed, sweetie. Are you hungry? We could have a nice little picnic. We could even have some fowl, I know you probably don't get much of that."

"...Alright. That sounds fun, Mut." And so it went. It was so odd, seeing her again, I almost didn't know how to act. She seemed happy enough just being with me, and that eventually made me loosen up.

The food was delicious—of course, I wasn't sure if it was real or not. I knew it was real for my Mwt, but she had already passed on. Was the food of the dead also food for the living? I wasn't sure, and I didn't want to ask with Osiris there for fear that I would get some sort of lecture...which would probably result in some sort of fight. No need to upset my Mwt.

We spent what felt like hours together, just talking about nothing. But when I mentioned Amahté in an offhand comment, she wasn't so casual.

"Amahté? Who is that, baby girl?"

"Hmm? Oh, he is...courting me."

"You are courting someone? Fala, I'm so happy for you! I wish I could meet him! Is he good to you? How long have you known each other? Does he have any family that I would know?"

"Um... his parents' names are Miu and Khenti."

"Oh. I know him. He's very, um, outgoing."

I laughed. "Mwt, you don't have to pretend to like him. I know I don't."

At that, she looked relieved. "Yes, he's a bit difficult to deal with. Osiris told me that he had twins. Which one are you courting?"

"Amahté is the one with the lighter skin and the darker hair. He's technically the younger one, though not by much. Maybe you can meet him someday."

"No."

I rolled my eyes. Of course, Osiris had to be the downer. "And why is that?"

"He would die if he came here. The only reason that you are safe is because you are my daughter." I am not ashamed to admit that I pouted at that. I had really wanted Amahté to meet my Mwt. "And speaking of the world of the living, we must head back. You can only stay here for so long because you are half human."

"...Fine." I said my goodbyes to my Mwt, trying to prolong them as much as I could. It was clear that Osiris and I weren't going to get along well for a long while—or maybe never—so I didn't know when I was going to see her again. When we finally headed back to the realm of the gods, I almost wished that I hadn't gone. The darkness was even more oppressive, and it felt like there was something pulling from inside of me, trying to keep me in the afterlife.

But then we arrived back in Osiris's estate, just as suddenly as we had gone. I breathed a sigh of relief; it was definitely worth the experience to see my Mwt, but that was by no means something that I wanted to do often.

After a moment, I realized that Osiris had yet to remove his arm from around my shoulder. "You can let go now," I said, "I'm not going to disappear. It's not like I have anywhere to go…" He frowned, but listened to me anyway.

"Is there anything that you need, Fala?" he asked.

I opened my mouth to make a snippy retort, but then closed it again. He *had* just taken me to see my Mwt. With the way I had greeted him, he could just have easily locked me in here all alone. "…No. I don't need anything."

He smiled brightly at me. "I am glad. If you are in need of anything, there are plenty of servants about. Please let them know."

"Are you going somewhere?"

He sighed. "Unfortunately. I must go deal with Khenti. He has overstepped his bounds greatly, and he must know it. I do not trust him." Huh. Well that was one thing that we could both agree on. "If you could please be back here slightly before sunset, I would like very much to dine with you."

Did I even have a choice? "…Fine."

He nodded, and leaned in to give me a kiss on the forehead. I backed away. "Fala?"

"I just met you," I told him, irritated. "You haven't been there for my entire life." When he started to object, I quickly added, "Whatever your reasons might have been, *I don't know you*. I'm not going to let us turn into one happy family just because we're in the same house now."

"Estate," he corrected, sighing and stepping away. "I must go now. You are free to wander where you wish."

"Alright." I was determined to remain cold. I wanted him to know that I was going to really stand by what I had said, that he would have to earn my trust. But the pitiful look he had in his eyes when he turned away made me call reluctantly, "I'll see you later."

That seemed to be enough. He smiled at me and left.

I sighed and headed over to the wardrobe. I was still in my clothes from yesterday, and while they weren't *that* dirty, I still wanted to clean up. I felt kind of disgusting, wearing the same thing two days in a row.

I stopped and laughed out loud. Ra, I was becoming so spoiled! What were the twins doing to me?

Still, I began looking for something to change into. These clothes were so different from anything I'd ever seen! There were long tunics with sleeves that went to my elbows in colors I had never even seen before. I chose one that I recognized. It was an earthy brown, with black, orange, and dusty green zigzagging across the bottom. It was long enough to wear without leggings, and it was light and comfortable.

I headed out and began to wander. I had no idea how long I was going to be staying here—even if it didn't take long to get the amulet out of my body, Osiris might try to keep me here. And while I appreciated being away from Khenti, I certainly didn't want to be away from the twins for long.

Although Osiris's estate certainly seemed nicer than Khenti's. It was colorful, and the walls were bordered with beautiful hieroglyphs. Every so often there was a gorgeous bouquet of flowers in an expensive-looking vase. The doors to the rooms were simple and elegant, something that I greatly appreciated. Some of the doors were locked, but most of them were open and uninteresting. I found a library, a kitchen, and several offices and spare bedrooms.

It was actually pretty nice here. I still wasn't a fan of my new room—it was drowning in frills and pink things—but the rest of the estate was…homey. It was a welcome change.

And as I passed many of the servants, I couldn't help but notice that they all seemed well taken care of. They were all well-dressed and clean, and they looked healthy and happy. Well, mostly happy. A lot of them got jittery and jumpy as soon as they saw me, but I figured that was simply because they had never seen me before. If I saw a random person walking around, I would be wary, too.

Eventually, I turned to go back. I was hungry, and I didn't want to be late for any food Osiris had to offer.

"Ah…Miss Fala?"

Oh, it was a servant. He was small and twitchy, and he wouldn't meet my gaze. "You can just call me Fala," I told him. Maybe that would help him feel better.

Instead, it only seemed to make his twitching worse. "Oh, no, I cannot do that."

"…Why not? I don't mind, really."

He shook his head and bowed. "No, no, miss, I cannot. I am under orders, we all are. You are specifically to be called 'Miss' or 'Miss Fala'. That is all."

I started to protest, but at this point the poor man was twitching so badly that it looked like he might collapse at any moment. "...Fine. Is there something I can help you with?" I said it as gently as I could, but his eyes still began to bulge.

"Oh, no, miss, it is not help, no, I simply have a message for you." He bowed again and looked at me expectantly.

"Okay," I said slowly. "What is the message?"

"Master Osiris would like me to take you to him in the garden. He would like to eat with you."

I smiled. "Perfect. I was just walking back to meet him. If you would lead the way?"

He bowed once more and turned to lead me back through the hallways. When we got to the garden, though, he ran ahead. I couldn't help but stop and gape. This garden was even more impressive than the one at the twins' estate. The trees seemed to droop under the weight of their fruits, and their leaves created a perfect path of shade winding through the place. There were elegant stone statues, nearly hidden among the greenery, and Osiris sat in the middle of it all.

I walked over to him slowly. I saw him speak with the servant briefly, then shake his head and dismiss him.

"What was that about?" I asked as the nervous man

ran past me.

"That was Shai. If you have an issue with him or his orders, please tell me instead in the future. He tends to be quite…anxious. I am afraid that if you try to change his mind he may have a panic attack. Still, he is a very hard worker and I like him."

"Could you tell the servants that they can just call me Fala? I'm not a 'miss', not even close."

"I do not agree. I would not want them to offend you—"

"I worked as a farmhand," I said bluntly, "and I had no heritage to speak of. I'm used to being looked down upon, so I really don't think they could offend me if they tried. Maybe once I get used to…this, they can be more formal if they want, but for now…I just want to be Fala."

"…I will inform the servants that it is allowed. However, I will not force them, and I cannot guarantee that they will be comfortable enough to use your given name."

I nodded in approval. "I'm glad to see that you're treating your servants like actual people, unlike Khenti."

He flinched. "Yes, well…I could never treat them poorly. In some places servants are treated so badly that they die very quickly. If that had happened, then…I never would have had the privilege of meeting your Mwt." His voice grew quieter, and he added, "I could never treat them badly after that."

I smiled and sat down beside him. I was nowhere near thinking of him as Ab yet, but already I could tell that he was a good person. The least I could do was give him a chance. "What do we have to eat?"

He beamed back at me. "Your mother said pheasant was your favorite, so I had that made. But there is also fish and gazelle, if you would prefer that."

I chose the gazelle; I'd never had it before. I had fish all the time—it was cheap and abundant. The meal was actually very good. The meat practically melted in my mouth, and I was given a delicious set of fruits. By the time I had finished, I was filled to bursting.

I groaned when I looked over and saw that there was still a lot of food left. "I can't eat that all!"

"Do not worry about it, Fala."

"But it's such a waste…" I had to be so frugal at home. To see so much food just sitting there was almost agonizing.

"The servants will eat it when it is taken back to the kitchens. Do not worry, nothing will go to waste." That, at least, made me feel better.

We sat in silence for a few minutes. I wasn't sure if I was supposed to do anything else, but it felt rude to just get up and leave without saying anything. So instead of leaving, I looked around and admired the garden. There were birds here, I realized, flitting through the trees as I watched. Everything was so…calm. It was nice here.

"Do you like it?"

I turned to face Osiris. He seemed nervous again; this was ridiculous, he was a High God. He should be able to handle little old me. "It's very…peaceful. It's nice."

"I am glad," he smiled. "Ah…you did not seem very happy with the room, however. If you would like, I could surely have it redone to suit your tastes."

"Don't worry about that. I'm not going to be here much longer anyway." I wanted to get back to the twins, and I wanted to make a new home for myself. I couldn't do that if I stayed here. And honestly, I didn't feel comfortable here. It was nice, but even the little bit of contact I'd had with the servants had left me feeling awkward and out of place.

"You…are leaving? Is there anything I could do that would make you wish to stay?" He sounded desperate now, pleading. Now I felt like a jerk for leaving him. "I am certain that we could go visit your Mwt more often, if you would like."

"No, no," I said quickly. "That's not what this is about. I just…I don't *belong* here. I want to make a home for myself, back in Egypt. I love Egypt, I could never leave it behind forever." Osiris was trying hard to be kind, I could tell, but if things were going to be this tense and awkward whenever he was around, then I wanted to get out as soon as possible.

Osiris sighed, and looked to the sky. "So much like Teanna," he whispered. Then he looked back to me and added, "I suppose I cannot stop you then." He stood and offered his hand to help me up, saying, "I must be going. I shall meet with you tomorrow, and then…then we can remove the amulet." He drooped a bit. "Then you may leave."

I bit my lip as he walked away. He seemed so sincere,

but I just did not want to stay here for the rest of my life. Maybe I could talk to him about coming to visit. That seemed like a fair trade. I could get to know him better, he could get a little insight into my life, and I would get to see both my Ab and my Mwt.

We definitely weren't a family in my eyes, not yet. But…maybe someday.

I sighed. It was getting late; the sun was nearly finished setting. I should get back to my room. I took a few steps towards the door before I realized something.

I didn't know where my room was! "Osiris!" No response. Not that I had really expected one, but I had been hoping. What was that servant's name again? The twitchy one? "Shai!" No luck there, either. I walked into the estate, cursing. How was I supposed to magically know where everything was in this house? Sure, I had walked around a little, but that didn't make me an expert!

I set off, hoping that at least I would run into someone who could point me in the right direction. I didn't see anyone; had everyone else already retired for the night? Where were the people when I needed them?

I tried a few doors, but they were already all locked. Had the servants done that? I hoped that they locked my door thinking that I was already inside.

No, that wasn't possible. I had only been wandering around for a few minutes. There was no way that was enough time for them to lock all of these doors, and they certainly couldn't expect me to be that fast. Right?

Of course not. I sighed. I was spending too much time thinking when I *should* be trying to find someone to lead me back to my room. …Or my room itself. You know, whichever came first would be fine by me.

"Hello?" I called out. "Is anyone there? I'm kind of lost…" I didn't get a response. Seriously? As soon as the sun set there weren't any servants anywhere? They all just disappeared?

"Hello?" I called out again, peeking behind a door. There wasn't anyone in here, either, but a painting along the back wall caught my eye. I moved in closer, squinting.

It was a painting of my Mwt and Osiris. They were standing there, looking into each other's eyes, and they were both smiling. My Mwt looked happy, and Osiris simply looked carefree with his arms wrapped around Mut. It was easy to see that they were in love.

Well, this was going to make things harder. I had intended to make Osiris work to be my Ab; I felt like he didn't have the right to just walk into my life and settle in. But seeing them so content made me *want* to let him in.

"Fala?"

I turned my head, my fingers halfway to the beautiful painting. "Ah…hello, Osiris."

He looked confused. "What are you doing in here? I thought that you would be headed back to your room."

"Yes, about that," I said, moving to face him fully. "I got lost. I was just wandering around and I found…this." I gestured back at the painting. "It's very beautiful."

"Yes," he said softly. "We did not know it at the time, but when that painting was done she was already nearly two months pregnant with you."

"Oh." I looked back once more at it. It seemed sad now that I knew it was only months before their separation. "I'm sorry." I didn't know what I was apologizing for, but it felt like the right thing to do.

Osiris put a hand on my shoulder. "Do not be sorry, Fala. I am glad that you were born, and I know that Teanna loves you very much. Neither of us would trade your life for the world."

I smiled at him, but I didn't need him to tell me that. I already knew it. My Mwt *had* given up her world for me.

He sighed and guided me toward the door. "Let us get you back to your room, shall we? Tomorrow we can work everything out." I nodded and let him lead me away.

I didn't sleep well that night. I couldn't figure Osiris out, and it made nervous. Not to mention the fact that I didn't know how to act around him. Should I try and stay cold, like I had originally intended? Or should I give him an honest chance?

Eventually, I drifted off into a fitful sleep, but that didn't last long. Before I could get much rest, Shai was knocking on my door.

"Miss? Miss, please, if you could get up. Master Osiris would like to speak with you. If you could just get ready..."

I rolled over and moaned. "Fine, fine, I'm up."

"Thank you, miss. I will just be outside."

I heard the door close behind him. This was just too early to be up. But I had no doubt that Osiris wouldn't let me sleep, so I pulled myself out of bed.

A set of clothes had been laid out already at the foot of my bed. I hadn't even noticed anyone come near the bed; that scared me a little bit. I didn't like knowing that people could get so close to me without my knowing. Still, this meant that I didn't have to worry about finding clothes. I decided to ask Osiris about it when I saw him.

Soon enough, I was ready. I stuck my head out the door, squeaking a little in surprise when I saw that Shai was standing right there. "Uh, I'm ready now. We can go."

He bowed and began to lead me through the hallways without a word. I tried to memorize the way as we went along, but by the time we reached Osiris's office I had forgotten all but a few hallways. Why was this place so confusing?

"Master Osiris. I have brought Miss Fala, as you had asked."

Osiris smiled. "Thank you, Shai. You are dismissed." When the servant had gone, Osiris turned to me and said, "Did you sleep well, Fala?"

"Yes, thank you." Did he really call me all the way out here just to ask me how I had slept? If that was everything, then I was *not* going to be happy. "Is there anything else?"

"Yes. I am getting you a tutor. I have a few options here, and I would like you to help me pick one." He smiled at me, as if I should be glad about this.

Instead, I was annoyed. "Why do I need a tutor?" I told

him.

"Did you have any formal education in the human world?"

"No."

"Then you need this," he insisted. "It is very important for you to be educated."

"I don't need that," I said. I hadn't been formally educated, but my Mwt had taught me the basics. I knew what I needed to know, and that was enough. Honestly, what was I going to be doing back in Egypt that I would need to know everything?

Osiris looked like he was torn between confusion and anger. I took a deep breath; I didn't want to get into an argument. I just needed to make him see that this really wasn't going to do me any good.

And there wasn't much time for us to argue anyway. A servant came running into the room before we got the chance.

"Master...Osiris," he panted, "there is... a demigod here... to see you...he goes by... Amahté, son of Khenti?" Oh, great. Now my lover was attempting to charge my Ab's house.

"Is that someone you know, sweetie?"

I rolled my eyes. "My name is *Fala*, and yes, I do know him." Turning to the messenger, I added, "Would you lead me to him?" He nodded, and I followed him through the maze of hallways, hoping that I could get to Amahté before he caused too much trouble.

"I don't care if he's busy! Where is Fala?" Too late. Amahté had a way of causing trouble—it was like a freakish talent that he had. I ran ahead of the frightened servant, following Amahté's voice. I slid around a corner and there he was, looking angrier than I had ever seen him.

"Amahté!" I called. He turned, and as I watched all the anxiety drained from his face. Did he really think that I was so incapable of taking care of myself? Still, it was sweet that he was so worried about me. It made me feel like I really *belonged*.

"Fala? What are *you* doing?" Osiris had caught up with me, and now he looked worried, and more than a little angry. Oh, *now* he decided to try and be an Ab.

"I'm hugging Amahté. We *are* courting," I said matter-of-factly. He could learn to deal with it; he hadn't been there for my whole life, so he didn't get any say now.

"You cannot court him! I will not allow it! Do you know who he *is*, Fala? His Ab is—"

"A complete jerk. I know that, but Amahté is fantastic. He's nothing like his Ab, and you have no right to say anything about it!"

"He is not good for you! He will only hurt you—"

"Hurt me?" I shrieked. "*He* is the one who will hurt me?! Don't you *dare* say that. You have hurt me more than anyone else in this world or the next! *You* left my Mwt, *you* let her die, *you* made my life hell! No one in this world could possibly cause me any more pain than *you*!"

I had always been good at repressing my feelings. An

outsider doesn't have the luxury of tears. But I had been through too much, too fast, and now the tears came. I tried to hide my face, tried to stop the rivulets running down my cheeks, but the tears just kept coming. I was too angry to stop them.

"Fala?" Amahté asked, panicked. He turned to Osiris, suddenly angry again. "Now look what you did!"

"I?" Osiris scoffed. "I have done nothing. It is you who has caused her tears; she would be fine if you had not shown up!"

"Don't blame this on me! I wouldn't have to worry about showing up if you hadn't taken her!"

"I was merely protecting her! She was not well-cared for under your Ab!"

Of course, the arguing only made things worse. Amahté realized it before Osiris did. He reached over and put his arm around me tightly. I didn't pull away. He turned us to the door and started to lead me away.

"Wait," Osiris said wearily. He closed the small distance between us, and put his hand on my arm. "Please do not leave," he told me. "He may stay here, if you wish it. Please." I didn't want to stay, but I really didn't think that I was up to traveling right now. And if I stayed here, I didn't have to deal with Khenti…

"Okay," I hiccupped, "okay." Osiris looked relieved. Reluctantly, he turned and began to lead us back through the house.

By the time we got back to the room, I had managed

to subdue my tears into sniffles. I felt like such an idiot. I had *never* lost control like this, and now I was a blubbering mess. Amahté and Osiris were going to think that I did this all the time—they didn't know any better, even Amahté hadn't known me long enough to see otherwise. The thought of my foolishness triggered another round of tears, this time from embarrassment. Amahté held me close, offering me comfort.

There was a slight step up from the hallway into the room. When I raised my foot to step into it, I almost fell over. Amahté caught me, but I needed his help to stay upright. My mind and my body had been under so much stress lately, and I hadn't been eating right. And my little breakdown didn't help.

Amahté saw that I was about to collapse and picked me up. I started to protest, but he shushed me with a quick, sweet kiss. He sat on the bed, pulling me against his chest, and I let his heartbeat lull me to sleep.

~*~

When I woke, I kept my eyes closed. My dreams had been so sweet—I didn't want to let go. But, soon enough, awareness took the place of dreams.

Reluctantly, I opened my eyes. Osiris wasn't there— that was a pleasant surprise. I had half-expected him to stand watch over my bed, especially with Amahté here. I tried to sit up, only to find that Amahté had fallen asleep with his arms wrapped around me. Oh, that was so sweet...highly inconvenient, but still sweet.

"Amahté," I whispered, placing a light kiss on his cheek. "Amahté, I need to get up."

"Ngh…why?" he said, his eyes still closed. "Stay here. Stay with meeeee…"

I laughed. "You sound like a child," I told him. But the idea didn't sound that bad. As much as I hated to admit it, I was still completely drained from yesterday. It would be nice to have a day to just sit around and do nothing—that never happened. Even at Khenti's estate, I had been running all over the place trying to find something to do or (to Amahté's dismay) helping the servants clean the place up. I wasn't exactly an idle person.

"I know," he said, propping himself. "We will not leave this room today. We will sit around and do nothing…except maybe play a few games because I get bored easily."

"What is that, a command?"

"Yes! The almighty Amahté commands that he and Fala do nothing today but little fun things!"

I rolled my eyes. "I suppose I could obey that particular command, oh 'almighty Amahté'. Now, what should we do first?" He looked completely baffled at that. This was going to be an interesting day if he couldn't even think of how to start. "How about some breakfast?"

"Um, yes! That is exactly what I was thinking! …But I think you'll have to be the one to ask for it. Lord Osiris doesn't seem to like me very much."

"Hmm, I wonder if that has anything to do with the fact

that you stormed his house. Or maybe it was when you started screaming in his face? Or maybe—"

"Alright, Fala, I get it… he has every reason not to like me. Can we have food? Pleeeeeeeeaaase?"

"Fine," I laughed. "I'll ask for some. But for the love of Ra, stop acting like you are five years old!"

"Mmm…I'm only acting that way because you are distracting me," he purred.

I blushed. He could be such a loser sometimes, but it was nice. I leaned in to give him a well-deserved kiss—

—So of course someone knocked.

"Come in," Amahté sighed. I sighed, too, and he bent towards me and whispered, "Later." I nodded, and pulled away from him just as the door opened.

"Yes?" he asked. The servant girl didn't respond; she was looking at me.

"What do you want?" I said. Okay, so I wasn't as formal as Amahté. Before I'd met him, the most formal thing I did was go to the temple. Specifically, the Temple of Isis, and had gotten kicked out of that. Reconstruction was still going on…two years later…

The girl seemed startled by my informality. Hadn't Osiris said that he would warn them about that? "Um…Master Osiris would like to know when you plan to come outside."

"Ugh…you can tell him that today is my day to do nothing. Today I am the mummy and this room is my tomb, Ra-dammit!" If she was startled before, she was shocked now. She nodded quickly and left. I turned to Amahté.

"That was awfully harsh, love," he said lazily. "You're going to scare all the poor servants."

"That's fine. They won't have to deal with me much longer, anyway. Now, where were we?"

~*~

"Roll over," Amahté commanded.

We were still in the bedroom. We had eaten lunch, played some board games, gotten yelled at by Osiris through the door…but mostly we just talked. It was nice to have a day where nothing was expected of you but some idle conversation.

I rolled over as he had asked, and he sat on my back. I started to ask what he was doing when he dragged his elbow down my spine. It felt *so* good. I began to relax as he continued to give me the best (and only) massage I'd ever had. When he had finished that, he sighed.

"Fala," he scolded gently, "your feathers are all ruffled." I shied away, but his hands were already on my wings, smoothing them, playing with the feathers. His tail wrapped around my legs, and I giggled. "What?"

"You're tickling me with your tail," I laughed. I heard him chuckle, and he went back to playing with my wings.

After a while, he lay down next to me, stroking my hair. "Love," he said softly, "why did Osiris bring you here? Has he treated you poorly?"

"I think I would almost prefer that. He has been almost annoying." I snorted. "He called me 'sweetie' yesterday."

Amahté sat up abruptly. "What? He's too old for you!"

I laughed. "Calm down, Amahté. He didn't mean it like that…I didn't get the chance to tell you before."

"Tell me what?"

I suddenly found the ceiling very interesting. "Weeeeell," I began, tapping my fingers together nervously, "I *may* have had another vision, and that vision *may* have had my Ab in it, and my Ab *might* be Osiris."

He stared at me. I waited for him to say something, but when he only continued to stare, I was afraid that I had sent him into shock. "…Amahté? Are you okay?" I reached over to pat his shoulder. "Ah…my Mwt was still human, you know. It's okay."

"Just—" He stopped and shook his head. "I just…don't even know anymore. I shouldn't be surprised, but…" He cut himself off again.

"I don't intend to stay here, you know." When he looked at me questioningly, I continued, "I want to go back to Egypt eventually. I'm just not sure if I could…What would Osiris think? And what would I do about your parents, and Akori?"

"Forget them."

I blinked, startled. "Forget them?"

"Why not? I can teach you to hide your wings, and we can go live in Egypt together. Just the two of us." I sat for a moment, stunned.

But he was right—that would be perfect. I didn't want to be involved in the affairs of the gods. I wanted my simple life back, and I wanted to be with Amahté. And if I could be with Amahté without ever seeing Khenti again, that would be even better. The best part was, I wouldn't have to forget about Akori; I was sure that, if Amahté left, he would come too.

Without a word, I got up and began to pack.

Chapter Eight

"Where will we go?" I didn't want to go back to the pit that had been my hometown, and even if I did the people there would condemn us as witches or demons. We would make a quick stop at my former home to take what we needed, and then we could move somewhere else.

"What about somewhere near the palace? That would be closer to the kind of the place you'd want to live, and it would be safer."

I agreed that would be a good idea. Honestly, I didn't care where we lived. I had lived in some bad places before, and I knew how to get through it.

"We'll have to fly out," Amahté warned me, "and I can't carry you the whole way."

"As long as you guide me, I should be fine," I said, remembering my flight with Kemreit. It was certainly good to know that I really would be fine; it was nice to have Amahté there, but I wanted to be able to take care of myself.

We grabbed only what we could carry, which wasn't much, but we could work for anything else that we needed. We were just about to leave through the window when there was a knock at the door.

"Fala? Fala, are you going to come out?" Of course, it just had to be Osiris. He had opened the door and walked in before he had finished speaking.

"You know," I said, "it's polite to wait for an invitation *before* walking in." When he didn't seem fazed, I added, "What if I had been *naked*?" At that, I was pleased to see him cringe. I couldn't help it—but I thought that I deserved a little sadistic pleasure. He got to mess with my life. Why couldn't I mess with his head a little?

Any pleasure I might have felt at his reaction faded when he saw our packed bags. The expression on his face made me remember that, even if he seemed helpless sometimes, he was someone to be feared.

"*What* are you doing?" he hissed.

There was nothing I could do to hide it now. "Well, obviously we're leaving."

"And just where are you leaving to?"

"I don't know that yet. But you can bet that it will be somewhere far, far away from here."

"He will not be able to take care of you properly! I am your Ab, I can—"

"You can what? You're not my Ab! Abs protect you, and support you, and they make sure the ones you love aren't taken from you! You haven't done any of those things! The only thing you've done is ruin my life, you—"

"Fala, you should not be so rude." I knew that voice—Akori was here!

"Where did you come from?" Amahté nearly tackled his brother, he was so excited. "Wait! Mwt and Ab aren't here, are they?"

"It is just me…for now. When I left, they had been packing. Now, Fala, how are you?"

"I have been better."

"Fala! When you are finished with your conversation, I was not done speaking to you."

I rolled my eyes. "Osiris, you have never done anything for me. Why should I do anything for you?"

Osiris opened his mouth to respond, but he was interrupted by a panicked servant. "Sir! Sir! There is an intruder in the south wing. We cannot track him!"

As the servant stood there anxiously, Osiris turned to me and said, "You don't want to listen to me? Fine. We will finish this later." With that, he muttered some incoherent spell and left, the servant trailing behind him.

I closed the door behind him, then turned to face the twins. "Let's go."

"That's impossible."

"What? Why? He doesn't need to know we're leaving."

Akori rolled his eyes. "Fala, that was a binding spell. It keeps you from leaving the property until the caster—in this case, Lord Osiris—removes it." He pointed to my collarbone, and I looked down to find that my 'bruise' was no longer blue. Now it was a purplish-red color, and it seemed to be glowing slightly.

"So…we can't leave?"

Amahté laughed. "Not unless you want to be paralyzed until Osiris decides otherwise. And trust me, you don't want that—it leaves a terrible aftertaste." Akori pretended to be stern for a moment before both of them burst out laughing. I couldn't help but join in; their laughter was so infectious!

After we had caught our breath, we sat down on the bed, and Akori asked, "So, have you decided where you want to live yet?"

"We've already decided that we will live around Abydos," I said. "I've always wanted to go there, and I have heard that it's amazing."

"And it's a busy city, so I will *have* to keep myself in check," Amahté laughed.

For a while, we just sat like that, enjoying each others' company. I wasn't quite ready to leave the lazy day behind me.

Akori was the one to finally break the silence. "Fala, if Osiris is your Ab, then he will have a responsibility to tell Mwt and Ab."

"Eh, that's not my problem. I don't care if Khenti knows."

"Yes, I am aware of that, Fala, but they will expect children."

I shrugged. Children would be nice, but I wasn't going to rush into something just for Khenti's sake, or even Miu's. That would be mine and Amahté's decision, and ours alone.

"...Fala?"

Wow, that sounded pitiful. "Amahté?"

"Perhaps we should not have children. I don't think that I could deal with children, and if we had twins everyone would expect—"

"I don't care what people expect," I told him bluntly. "If we end up having children, and we have twins, everyone can go get eaten by crocodiles for all I care. If we're living in Egypt we won't have to live by the rules of the gods."

"That's true…" But he still seemed hesitant. That was alright—I just needed to get him used to the idea.

Amahté and I shared the bed that night. Akori used a nearby reclining couch. Poor Akori—he never got the bed! I felt badly, but he had insisted. He said it was only right that the two "lovebirds" (as he called us) shared the bed.

Amahté was snoring contentedly beside me, but I couldn't fall asleep. I was too excited about the new life that we would have together. I wanted to get out of here as soon as I could, but I was still bound.

There was one other thing troubling me, although I would never admit it to the twins. The servants had been rushing about all evening, crying frantically for medicine and bandages. Who was hurt? Was it Osiris? I was still angry with him—I felt like I had a right to be—but he *was* my Ab. I couldn't help but worry.

And what would happen if there was no god of the dead? What would happen to those who had already passed, or to those who were still living?

"Miss Fala?" a girl called through the door. Oh, gods,

here was my answer. She was probably here to tell me who had been hurt. But I had wanted to know, hadn't I? I disentangled myself from Amahté's embrace and went to get the door. The servant on the other side had a look of panic on her face.

"Has something happened?" I asked, although I knew the answer was yes. I had to start somewhere.

"Miss Fala...Master Osiris has sent for you. He is badly hurt and he wants to speak with you immediately."

"How bad are his wounds?"

"He...may not make it through the night." I took a deep breath to steel myself and went to wake the twins.

"Huh—? Whazzat?"

"Amahté, get up, we have to go. Osiris is hurt—he might be dying!" *That* woke him up.

"You can go on ahead; I'll wake Akori." I didn't need to be told twice. I rushed out after the servant even as I heard Akori begin to get up.

The hall seemed to stretch on forever. Door after door, I expected to stop, but we didn't. Finally, we came to the end of the hallway. I stopped for a moment just outside the door, trying to prepare myself.

I wasn't prepared enough. Osiris was lying on a medical table in the middle of the room, pale as the moon at midnight. The table looked eerily like an embalming station. I shivered, not wanting to think about it, and moved closer. That made it even worse; there was blood all over him, and more was leaving his body every second. How is it that a god could look so fragile—!

But when I looked closer, I realized that this wasn't a simple wound at all. His arms looked mutilated, and there was a gash in his chest that would have killed even the strongest of humans instantly. His head was swathed in blood-soaked bandages, and he was barely breathing.

The room spun a little, and Amahté reached out to steady me. When had he gotten here?

"Ngh…" Osiris opened his eyes slowly. They were cloudy, distant. One of the physicians in the room motioned for me to move closer.

"Osiris?" I said softly. "…Ab?" His hazy eyes travelled to me for a moment, and he reached weakly for my hand. I gave it to him without any complaint. He muttered something that I couldn't make out, and I said, "Don't try to talk…"

He shook his head. "For…you," he breathed out. "Only…wanted you…to be happy…be happy, Fala…go…love…you…"

His hand fell limp and his eyes closed once more, his breathing more ragged than ever.

"He unbound you," Akori whispered gently. "You can leave whenever you want."

I moved slowly towards the door, not wanting to leave my Ab but knowing that I had to. The twins let me run past them.

How could someone *do* this? Osiris was a pain sometimes, but he seemed like he only had everyone's best interests at heart. And who could possibly be strong enough to kill a god?

I shook my head. No, not kill. He would be fine. He would recover, and then we would go see my Mwt tomorrow. Everything would be fine—

"Ha!"

I turned, startled, and suddenly there was a blinding pain in my shoulder. What was happening?! Without thinking, I grabbed my shoulder, but then the pain was in my hand, too. I looked down and had to fight the urge to throw up. There was an arrow sticking *through* my shoulder…and it had cut up my hand too. What in Ra's name?

"You're his daughter, aren't you? Well, a pretty little thing like you shouldn't be running around alone…"

I staggered a bit, then turned to face my attacker. Who was this? I had never seen him before in my life—what was he doing here?

Was he the one who had attacked my Ab?

"Now then, would you like to die by my bow—" He held up the bow still in his hand— "or by my sword?"

Well this would be fun. He had two weapons and I had nothing. Unless…

"If I had to pick," I said, trying not to show how much my shoulder was hurting me, "I'd choose to fight you up close. Can't you handle me without a weapon, you coward?"

He laughed, but dropped his bow. "Spunky! I like that." Without any warning, he charged at me, screaming.

I barely had enough time to rip the arrow from my shoulder and thrust it in front of me—straight into his chest.

But it didn't even seem to slow him down; he just batted me aside.

I stumbled back, trying not to fall. If I fell, it was all over, I would be at his mercy. "Monster," I spat. "What do you want?" If I could just buy some time, then I could have a chance.

But he didn't seem to even hear me. He pulled the arrow out of his flesh, dropping it to the ground, and reached for his sword. I backed away—I still didn't have a weapon. Why hadn't I held on to that arrow…

He charged me again, still bleeding. I dodged him, praying to any god that would listen that maybe, just maybe, his wound would take its toll. I turned to run, hoping that I could lead him outside. If I could get him outside, then I could fly up, and I would have the advantage.

Well he wasn't going to let *that* happen. Before I had taken even a few steps, he had grabbed my wing and yanked me back, down to the ground. He hadn't been that close when I turned—how was he so fast?

I tried to sit up, but he put his foot down on my throat. Why was he so *strong*? What was he?

"I didn't think I'd get to kill you, too—I thought it was only the god I would get. I bet I'll get a nice bonus for you."

A bounty hunter? No, that couldn't be right! How could a bounty hunter do so much damage?

"My master will be pleased to hear that I've finished my work," he sneered, pressing even harder on my throat. I tried to push his foot away, but I couldn't move it. He was just too strong… "He was angry last time. I managed to kill your Mwt, but you were left behind. You sneaky little bitch…"

What?! Why would anyone want to do that? My Mwt had never heard anyone…

The knowledge that he had killed my Mwt, and quite possibly my Ab, gave me strength. I threw him off of me, and dashed to the other side of the room, coughing. As I moved away, though, he lashed out with his sword and cut across my knee.

He was laughing. "Isn't this fun, little one?"

"W-why," I wheezed, "why would you want to kill my Mwt?"

His laughter stopped, but the insane grin remained. "I don't know. I don't care. Master Set wanted it, and so it was."

Set? Wasn't that…Osiris's brother? Dear Ra, would this never end? The gods should just learn to get along—at this rate, they would all destroy each other, and then where would the rest of us be?

"So you're Set's lapdog?" I said. This was stupid—I was bantering with a man who wanted to kill me! But I couldn't think of anything else to do. My shoulder was still bleeding, and it was taking its toll. I didn't think I could move my arm properly if I needed to. And forget about running; my knee was destroyed. How could I win this fight?

The answer was simple: I couldn't, not with my injuries. The best I could hope for was to hold him off until someone else came to my rescue.

Ugh. Even in my head, that sounded awful.

"Forget this," I muttered. "If I'm going to die, I'm taking you with me."

"What was that, pretty girl? I couldn't hear you. Let me come closer." And with that, he charged me again. This time, he came with the sword and a dagger that I hadn't even noticed. I jumped to the side, making a grab for the dagger with my injured hand. I couldn't afford to cut my good hand up.

He managed to land a blow on my arm, but I was able to hold onto his wrist with the dagger. I kneed him in the stomach as hard as I could, and when he flinched away I took the dagger. It wasn't a sword, but it was better than nothing.

This time, I charged him, aiming the knife for his neck. I had no other chance—this man was going to keep trying to kill me until he couldn't move anymore.

"There!" I had him—or at least, I thought I did. The dagger had definitely broken skin; it was covered in blood, and I had seen it go into his throat. But he was still moving! He was practically unstoppable!

"You have no chance," he ground out, blood spurting from his throat with every breath. He brought up the sword, slicing my already-wounded knee as I leapt away.

Could nothing stop this monster?

"Fala!"

"Ah…Akori? Where's Amahté?" I huffed. Breathing was getting harder now. I was losing too much blood, and my throat was already injured…

"Right *here*!" As he spoke, Amahté launched himself at my attacker's head, and Akori threw a dagger into his chest. For the first time, I saw the man stumble, and he seemed to struggle to stand back up. The twins' double attack had done the trick.

As Amahté leapt away, he grabbed onto the sword that had given me so much trouble, and with one strong pull it was away from the attacker.

It was over now. There were three of us against him, and he was wounded. No matter what type of monster he was, we had him now.

He seemed to come to that same conclusion. His glance shot between us before he laughed, a short, bitter bark that sent chills down my spine. "I always knew that it would end this way. Lord Set will not be pleased…" With that, he dropped to his knees. I breathed a sigh of relief. If he was giving up, then it would make this so much easier; I didn't want anyone getting hurt. I didn't know what I'd do if one of the twins ended up like Osiris…

"Fala, run!"

"What?" Why were we running? Wasn't he giving up? But then his body was bursting into flames, and those flames were targeting us.

Amahté grabbed me and pulled me along, with Akori right beside us. We ran as fast as we could, but I was falling behind. My knee was taking its toll—the flames were gaining on us.

"Come on, we can make it! The door's right around the corner!"

The corner—if we could make it around the corner and get the door closed, we could buy some time. We might even be able to get away completely.

"Akori, charm the door!"

Akori nodded and sprinted ahead, already chanting a spell. As he spoke, water began to rise around the corner and—I assumed—around the door, too.

We rounded the corner. Or at least, Akori and Amahté did. As I turned, I heard something snap, and I collapsed. My leg didn't want to move—I didn't want to die like this—!

Amahté whirled around and grabbed me, throwing me into the door right behind Akori. I turned around just as he closed the doors, just as he was engulfed in flames.

"*AMAHTÉ!!*" No, this couldn't be happening, Amahté couldn't die! I pulled frantically at the door, trying to get it open, but Akori pulled me back, sobbing.

"You can't open it," he cried. "The spell won't let you open it until the fire is gone…"

We could only listen, hoping against hope that the fire would subside soon. I pulled the door as soon as we heard it no more—it opened, the fire was gone. I dragged myself to Amahté's side; my knee had completely given out.

Amahté was barely breathing…I could barely recognize him…

"No," I cried softly. "Not again…not again…"

There was a knock at the door. I dropped the bucket and ran to my hiding place. People had been dying left and right, and my Mwt was worried. I was to hide until my Mwt said it was safe again.

Once I was hidden, she opened the door. I could only peek in horror as a sword came plunging through her body. There was cold, chilling laughter, and then I was alone.

"Mwt!" I cried, darting to her side.

"Fala," she said softly, "you were supposed to stay hidden. Why did you come out, baby girl?" I couldn't answer. I was crying too hard. I wrapped one arm around her, and held her with the other. I sat like that, listening to her voice, until it faded from her.

And she was gone.

My Mwt had been a brave woman. She had never fought in battle, but she had given up her life for me. She had given me safety at the cost of her own.

And now it was happening again!

"Amahté, Amahté," I cried. I tried to pick him up, to hoist him over my shoulder so that I could bring him to safety, but my leg just kept giving out. "Akori, help me!"

Akori didn't respond. He was silent, just staring in horror at his brother's mangled body.

"Akori! He's alive, we have to help him!"

"I...he can't be gone..."

"He isn't gone. For the love of Ra, help me, dammit!"

"Fala!"

I turned—Osiris! He was awake!

"Fala, what is going on? What happened to Amahté?"

"It was Set," I gasped. "Set sent someone to kill us—Amahté saved me—he's hurt, he's dying—you have to help him!"

Osiris stared at me, wide-eyed, before turning to someone behind him. "Isis, can you do anything?"

The woman—Isis—rushed ahead, and over to my side. "I will do what I can."

"Okay, what can I do?" I asked.

She looked up at me, briefly, before turning back to Amahté and saying, "*You* can go see Lord Osiris's physicians. You are no good to anyone with your injuries."

I started to protest, but then Osiris was at my side, pulling me up. "Come on, Fala. Amahté is in good hands."

"...Alright." I didn't like it, but I would only be in the way here. "Akori has to stay. He won't leave Amahté..." Isis nodded, but didn't say anything. Her hands were already moving over Amahté, leaving a soft, golden light in their trail. Osiris put my arm around his shoulder, and we began to walk away. "...Did she heal you?"

"Hmm? Yes. Isis is very skilled. I did not think she would get here in time...even she could not heal me fully. My leg is not fully healed, and my side still needs bandaging. Oh," he broke off, noticing my face, "Amahté will be fine. Magical burns are different."

We hobbled along in silence for awhile. I think that he didn't know what to say, and I was too worried about Amahté to think of much else. We finally made it to the physician's room, where I was whisked away from Osiris. It was overwhelming—I was suddenly surrounded by too many doctors to count, and none of them would talk to me.

As they were bandaging my shoulder, Osiris fought his way through to me. "You said Set did this? Set sent this man?"

"Yes."

He sighed. "When will he leave me be…" he said quietly, more to himself than to me. Then he looked up at me, and a frown marred his face. "I am sorry that I could not protect your Mwt from him."

"It's…fine." It wasn't fine, not really, but I could tell that he needed this, and I was willing to try and make this family thing work. "How long befo—ah! Be *careful*, Ra-dammit!"

The physician had yanked so hard on my wing—I was definitely going to be short a few feathers. "I'm sorry, miss, it had to be done."

When I only continued to glare at him, Osiris gently put his hand on my uninjured arm. "He is only doing his job, Fala."

"…I know."

The physicians seemed to take forever. More than once they had to ask me to sit still. I couldn't help being antsy. Amahté was hurt, maybe dying, and I was here getting poked and prodded by a group of people who didn't seem to understand what I was going through.

I had to look away when they fixed my knee. It had

been covered by my tunic, but when the physician pulled it back, I almost threw up. The bone was sticking out of my skin, and the whole thing was purple and bloody. No wonder it had hurt so badly—!

"I need to snap this back in, miss."

I nodded, biting my lip. Oh, Ra, this was going to hurt. Osiris reached over and took my hand, and when he squeezed my hand I gave him a small, pained smile.

"Ready? One, two—"

"Agh!" I jerked, and Osiris had to hold me in place. "Oh, Ra," I said, a single sob leaking out. Gods, why did it hurt so much now?

"It will get better, Fala," Osiris said soothingly, running his fingers through my hair.

"Why does it hurt so much now?"

"You were distracted before, so you did not feel the pain. It will get better now that it is fixed. It will be alright." I laid my head on his shoulder and took a deep, shuddering breath.

"Now, miss, I just need you to take this to help you sleep—"

"No."

"Miss, you need to rest—"

"I said no. I need to be with Amahté. I will rest after I know that he is going to be alright."

"Fala…" Osiris said. "I am sorry. But you are my first concern." I began to ask what exactly he intended to do, but he didn't let me finish. Instead, he chanted a spell that had me asleep almost before I knew what was happening.

I was going to be so mad when I woke up…

~*~

"Fala…"

"Ungh…wha…?" I opened my eyes slowly, wincing at the light.

"Hey, Fala." It was Akori, trying to smile, even though he looked like all he wanted to do was cry.

I sat up quickly—too quickly. My head spun. Still, I asked, "Amahté? Is Amahté alright?"

At that, the tears started to fall. "He's…he's in a room nearby. Isis did all she could, but…it's all up to chance now. We'll have to pray he makes it. I—" The tears broke free, and suddenly he was sobbing uncontrollably.

"Akori…" I pulled him into my arms.

"I—I don't kn-ow wh-what I'll d-do if he di-hiees!"

"Everything will be alright, Akori. Amahté's a fighter, he'll make it. But if you're really that worried, then why don't we go see him?"

He nodded, crying too hard to speak.

"Come on. Help me up, and we'll go find Amahté." Akori nodded once more, and pulled me up off the bed. I braced myself, expecting pain, but there wasn't any. My knee—along with my other injuries—seemed completely healed.

How could that have healed in only a night? Even

Osiris's physicians weren't that good—he *had* healed quickly, but I was only a half-god.

"Akori," I said slowly, "how long was I sleeping?"

He flinched, tears still on his cheeks. "I…you've been asleep for ten days. Lord Osiris said that would be best…"

"Ten…days?" So much could happen in ten days—that would be the difference between life and death for Amahté! How could they keep me asleep for that long? I let go of Akori; I didn't need to lean on him if I was healed. I grabbed him and pulled him along instead, looking through every door to find Amahté. The first door I flung open had a couple of servants behind it.

"Perfect!" I blurted. "Where's Amahté?"

They just stared at me blankly. "I…I do not know who that is, miss," one of them said.

"Oh, come on! He's a demigod, Isis was treating him for burns. I know he's here somewhere!"

"Oh," said the other one. "I do not know, miss. Lady Isis just ordered him to be moved. I do believe that he is in the next hall, toward the garden…" I spun and headed off, calling my thanks back over my shoulder. Once I got to the next hall, I only had to open a few doors.

When I did find him, my heart almost stopped. I could tell it was him, now, so that was an improvement. Before I wouldn't have known it was him if I hadn't been there myself. It could have been a complete stranger and I wouldn't have known the difference.

But that was where the improvements ended. Most of

his body was still swathed in bandages, and the skin that was peeking out between was definitely still burnt. There was a horrible stench filling the air—Isis's treatment for the burns, Akori whispered to me.

I moved to his bedside. His breathing was shallow, but it seemed better than it had the last time I saw him. I hoped that was true and not just wishful thinking on my part.

"He is much better than he looks, I can assure you." Isis was still here with him. Was that good or bad?

I tore my eyes away from Amahté's prone body. "Does that mean he's going to make it, Isis?" She wouldn't give me false hope. From what I had heard, she was much too frank for that.

"His chances are much better. I have healed his lungs, and that was my biggest worry. Now his skin is healing, and with continued assistance, I believe he will be alright."

I sighed. "Thank Ra…"

Isis hesitated, but looking at Akori's desperate face, she added, "Please do not count on it just yet. I will continue to do what I can, but young Amahté himself is the most important factor here. And things can always go wrong."

"Amahté will make it. He's a fighter," I said, as much for Akori's benefit as for mine. "He'll make it," I said again, taking his hand in mine. If he could just know that I was here, that Akori was here, maybe that would help him.

Isis simply bowed. "I have done all I can for today. I will be taking my leave. I was just finishing here."

"What?" I said. "I thought you said he still needed

care! How can you just leave him alone?"

"He cannot be given too much energy at once," she explained. "His body would become overwhelmed and he would most certainly die. I know that waiting is painful, but this is what is best for him."

I nodded slowly. She knew better than I did what Amahté needed. I just wished that there was more that I could do. Isis bowed once more, and left the room.

"Fala?"

I had never heard Akori sound so pathetic. He looked so desperate. "What is it, Akori? Do you need something?"

"I...if..." He stopped, taking a deep, shuddering breath to steady himself. "If Amahté doesn't make it..."

"He *will* make it, Akori, I know he will."

"But if he *doesn't*—I don't want to think about it either, Fala, but we have to—if he doesn't, then...can I move to Egypt with you? Amisi and I? We...I don't think we could make it under my Ab...without Amahté around."

"I..." Ra, I didn't want to think about this right now. I didn't even want to consider the possibility of losing Amahté.

But Akori was right. If things had been bad under Khenti before, they would be outright awful now. Khenti would blame Akori for Amahté's death. He would never have a moment of peace, and Amisi would go down with him.

"Of course, Akori. We should all try to stay together anyway."

We stood there in silence for a while. It just felt wrong to try to say anything at all, with Amahté suffering right beside us. And really, what was there to be said? We both knew what the other was thinking. We were praying for his survival, and that was all.

"May I come in?" Osiris was here.

"Come on in," I called, though I knew he would open the door before I finished speaking.

"I thought I would find you here, Fala," he said softly. "How are you feeling?"

"My injuries are all healed."

"That is not what I asked. I asked how you were feeling."

"I..." Oh, I couldn't do this. "I just want him to wake up."

"I know."

Akori spoke up then. "Lord Osiris, I... I am sorry for just bursting into your house like this. I mean no disrespect, I just...wanted to be near Amahté."

"That is perfectly alright. You two are twins, yes? That can be a very strong bond." It was sad to know that Osiris and his brother couldn't be that close.

"Lord Osiris...have our parents arrived yet?"

Oh, shoot. I had completely forgotten that Khenti and Miu were on their way. There was no way that I was going to put up with Khenti right now. Amahté was in so much pain—he needed to stay here, and Akori needed to stay with him. I knew that Khenti wouldn't be too happy about that, but I wasn't going to let him get in the way of Amahté's health or Akori's happiness.

"Yes, they arrived a short while ago, but…" Osiris hesitated. *That* worried me—even when he seemed anxious around me, he had never been hesitant. "I know that Set sent that man. That much you two were aware of."

"What else could there be?" I asked. Akori looked just as confused as I was.

"We…were making sure that there were no other intruders. I only wanted to keep you safe, Fala." Now he sounded like he was apologizing—that was really scaring me.

"Lord Osiris?" Akori looked just as frightened as I felt. "What does this have to do with Mwt and Ab?"

"I—" Osiris paused, then looked at Akori for the first time since entering the room. "There is…quite a bit of evidence to suggest that Khenti was working for Set. We believe that he led the attacker to this estate."

"No…" Akori looked devastated. "That—I mean, Ab didn't really approve, but he wouldn't…he couldn't have…"

"Akori!" I reached out to grab him just as he collapsed. "Are you sure?" I asked, looking back up at Osiris. I knew that Khenti was a schemer, but I didn't think he would go *this* low. How could he do that knowing that both his sons were here?

"There is no doubt," Osiris said. "Here, I will help you get him onto a bed. There is one in the next room."

I was about to protest, but Osiris picked Akori up like he weighed nothing. I stared after him for a moment—I was in fairly good shape, and Akori still wasn't easy for me to carry.

"I will take care of him," Osiris called back. "You stay

here with Amahté. I know that is where you want to be."

"…It isn't right to leave Akori all alone," I protested weakly, but he was right; I didn't want to leave Amahté's side.

"He will not be alone. There is a young woman here to see him; Amisi, I believe she said her name was?"

"…I see. That's good." Amisi would take care of Akori, and I could stay here with Amahté. Osiris nodded and left the room, carrying Akori with him, and I turned back to my wounded lover. "Come on, Amahté…I know you can do this. You can get through this."

I didn't even know if he could hear me. But if he *could* hear me, I needed him to know that I was there. I needed him to know that, even if he could not see me, he wasn't alone. Isis had said that Amahté was the most important factor in his own healing; I would do everything that I could to make sure that he had the will to live.

Besides that, I didn't want him to be here alone if his Ab showed up. Khenti had followed through on his threat to Akori—I was still here, still a problem, and he had tried to kill me. Sadly, I wasn't surprised that he had been willing to risk Akori's life. But Amahté's…I had thought that even he would be more concerned about Amahté.

I still couldn't believe that Miu had allowed this. I knew that she didn't treat Akori well, but it had seemed like she was not a supporter of physical violence of any kind. Maybe she hadn't known about it? But how could that be—she was with Khenti most of the time. Surely she had sensed that *something* was seriously wrong, even if he hadn't said anything.

"Oh, Amahté," I said softly. "What are we going to do with your family?"

I was sitting with him when I heard the screaming down the hall.

Before I really knew what was happening, Khenti had burst into the room, throwing Amisi to the ground in front of him. He was battered—he had probably tried to put up a fight when he knew that he had been caught.

His wild eyes flew over the room before landing on me. "*You*," he hissed. "You are the cause of all this!"

I stood, putting myself between Khenti and Amahté. Khenti looked absolutely insane, and he had to be desperate. In that state he might hurt even his favorite son. I would *not* let that happen; if I could take on Set's assassin, then I could *definitely* take on Khenti.

"I haven't caused anything, Khenti," I said slowly. "You brought this all on yourself. All you had to do was treat your sons the way they deserved to be treated."

"I did!" he growled, seeming more like a wild animal every moment. "I treated Wakhashem like the mongrel he is, and I gave Amahté everything! I showed him how to succeed, I gave him every opportunity to marry someone worthy of his name, and who does he choose?!" Amisi was crying now, trying to cover her head.

"He chose me—"

"He chose a worthless *bitch*, a daughter of a *whore*, and even the fool chooses a worthless human servant girl!"

He stepped forward, toward Amisi. I moved too, but in a split second I realized that I wouldn't get there in time. He was going to hurt her—!

Just as Khenti's foot was about to come down on Amisi's head, he was pulled back and literally thrown into the wall.

Akori was awake, and he looked livid. I couldn't remember ever seeing him so angry—so *frightening*. He had finally had enough.

"How *dare* you?" he hissed. "I have never done *anything* but try to please you. I have lived my entire life under your shadow, and I have stayed there to make you happy. And what have you done in return?! Nothing! You have belittled me and treated me like absolute shit!" His voice grew louder and more deadly with each second, and with every word he took a step closer to his Ab.

"You are—" Khenti began, but Akori stopped him with a kick to the stomach.

"And now you have the *audacity* to attack the woman I love?!" He took Khenti's head, and slammed it into the wall.

This had to stop—he was getting out of control, and as much as I loved to see Khenti get what he deserved, Akori would regret this later. "Akori, that's enough—"

"No!" he screamed, turning to face me. "I can't *do* it anymore, Fala! I want him gone, I want him out of my life for good!"

"Akori!" Amisi was up off of the ground now, holding onto her lover's arm. "Please, Akori...please stop...I know he has done you so much wrong, but if you do this you are letting him win. You are sinking to his level. Please…"

"No!" he screamed, turning to face her. Amisi flinched away from him, and that seemed to bring him back to his senses.

Slowly, his chest still heaving, Akori backed away. "Okay, Amisi…alright…" He sank to the floor—it seemed like he was drained, and he looked like he could pass out again at any moment.

"Akori?" I said softly. "Are you alright now?"

He nodded, holding Amisi close. "I'm sorry, Fala…" Khenti was still on the ground, trying—and failing miserably—to stand up again. His head was bleeding badly.

I sighed in relief, falling back on Amahté's bedside. "It's alright. I just didn't want you to regret this…" Just then, Osiris ran in. "You're a little late, At."

"Did you just call me At?"

I blushed when I realized that I had, in fact, called him 'At'. I wanted this family to work, and it was hard to ignore how much he wanted me to be safe and happy. "Well, you are, and I…well, we're just bonded by trauma."

"Fala, I do not…I am so—"

"Can we finish this later?" I interrupted. Now was *not* the time for him to turn into a pile of family mush. If Amahté could hear us right now, he was probably hoping for us all to shut up so he could rest. "Khenti just attacked us, he hurt Amisi, and he called my Mwt a whore."

At that, Osiris's eyes darkened. That was the

reaction I had been hoping for. Maybe we couldn't hurt Set, but now Khenti would be punished for sure, and I knew that as a High God, Osiris could do more to him than any of us.

He looked slowly from Khenti, still on the ground— trying to look submissive and innocent and failing horribly— to Akori and Amisi.

"Amisi is a human, yes?" he said slowly. We all nodded, although I wondered where that had come from. Osiris went to Khenti and pulled him to his feet. "You have made your disdain for humans quite clear...I hear that Lord Anhuri has been looking for a new servant at his palace."

"Lord Osiris—" Akori began, but Osiris continued without ever turning his burning gaze away from Khenti.

"Amisi needs to stay with her lover. I need to get rid of you. Losing your power should do both." At that, Khenti's eyes widened, and he began to struggle. He knew what was coming, and even if I didn't, it was good to see him squirm. But Osiris held him in his place. "Amisi, please come over here."

She stood and went to him, looking afraid but at the same time hopeful. "Yes, Lord Osiris?"

He turned his head briefly and smiled at her, but his eyes were cold. "All I need you to do is hold still."

She nodded, and Osiris began chanting a spell. Khenti began screaming as a bright light engulfed both him and Amisi—was it from pain or fear? It lasted for only a few seconds, but Khenti continued his cursing even after the light had faded. Amisi staggered backwards just as Osiris threw Khenti to the floor. Akori jumped up to catch her.

"Take him away. And contact Lord Anhuri...tell him that we have his new servant."

Two guards I hadn't even noticed began to drag Khenti away. We could still hear him screaming and cursing as Akori turned to Osiris and asked, "Lord Osiris, forgive me for being blunt, but what did you just do?"

Osiris smiled and moved towards the door, though his eyes were still cold. "I gave him a suitable punishment. I took away all of his powers and enhanced abilities as a demigod. I left his life force, however—he will live the next century as a human servant would live. Lord Anhuri has a reputation for treating his servants quite poorly...and I will stop by from time to time to make sure that he does not become too comfortable."

Comfortable—ha! There was no way that Khenti could ever be comfortable again, not if he had to live as a human. He would be completely miserable. I couldn't have picked his punishment better myself.

"What will happen to my Mwt?" Akori asked anxiously. "And why did you need Amisi?"

"Your Mwt and I have already spoken. She has asked to leave quietly and join Khenti in his banishment. I know for a fact that she was unaware of your Ab's plans, and so I will make sure she, at least, is somewhat taken care of." Poor Miu. I really felt that she had been dragged into all of this. If only she had married someone other than Khenti...but no, I couldn't say that. As much as I hated Khenti, without him, neither of the twins would have been born.

"But what about Amisi, At?" I said. He had said something about using Khenti's powers, but I didn't think I would ever understand all this magical exchange.

"I used his powers to create a new life force. Amisi is still human, but now she will age like a demigod."

Amisi and Akori stared at him for a moment, completely shocked, before blurting out thanks at lightning speeds. I didn't think it was possible for anyone to be so grateful, and they both looked happier than I had ever seen either of them.

I was happy for them, too. Now they didn't *have* to work around the age problem; they could simply live out their lives with each other. I looked wistfully at Amahté—we wouldn't have that problem, but if he didn't make it…

Osiris saw me, and raised his hands to cut the happy couple off. "You are both very welcome. But now, perhaps, we should leave Fala and Amahté alone."

Both of them nodded enthusiastically. Akori was probably too stunned to think about anything but Amisi right now.

Especially when Amisi grabbed his face and practically assaulted his lips with hers. "Come on, Akori," she said breathlessly. "We have somewhere else we need to be. Fala can take care of Amahté…I need *you* to take care of *me*." Giggling, she pulled him to his feet and out of the room.

Osiris stared after them for a moment before shaking his head. "That is something that I did *not* need to see."

Then he sighed, and turned back to me. "I am sorry that I cannot do more for him, Fala. I know how much he means to you."

"...It's alright." It wasn't Osiris's fault that Amahté had gotten hurt. "I'm the one he was trying to help. If he hadn't come to get me..."

"No, Fala," Osiris said softly, coming to my side. "You must not blame yourself for this. He made his choice, and that choice was to protect you at any cost. I know it is hard, and I know that you want him to be healed, but you must respect his decision."

I nodded, refusing to let the tears fall from my eyes.

He sighed once more, then backed away. "I need to pay Khenti a visit. I have not finished punishing him for calling my wife a whore..."

"Why didn't you do that here? Why have him taken away?"

He smiled brightly at me. "My dear, the things I intend to do to him are entirely unsuitable for children's eyes."

I stared at him, mouth wide open, until he left. *That* was unexpected. I turned back to Amahté. There was nothing I could do about it now...and this was one time that I actually didn't *want* to see Khenti punished. I felt like it could only end in disaster.

The weeks passed painfully slowly. Isis was constantly reassuring me that no matter how bad it looked, Amahté was recovering. I could see it now, even as untrained as my eye was. His hair was growing back, and the bandages were slowly being replaced by first burn cream, and then healed skin.

But he still hadn't woken up. At this point, the only thing keeping him from dying of starvation or dehydration was Isis's magic.

I didn't want to leave him, but I was always made to leave the room when the Isis was there. She said that my magic would interfere with his healing because I couldn't control it yet. That was something that I desperately wanted to fix, so I asked Osiris if he could find me a tutor. He replied that he would teach me himself.

During the first lesson, he tried to teach me to hide my wings. "The first thing that you need to do," he told me, "is remove the amulet."

I stared and him, then deadpanned, "At, it's still in my skin. You never took it out."

"Oh. You are correct. One moment, please." One short incantation later, the amulet was in his hand. I rubbed at my collarbone; it was strange, not having it on me. "Now, if you do not mind, you must close your eyes."

I did without any complaint. I knew absolutely nothing about magic, so I would just have to trust him.

"Now, I would like you to picture yourself the way you would like to look."

"Wait," I said, opening my eyes. "Does that mean that I can change the way my hair looks? My face? My skin?"

"Once you get more practice, it is possible to a certain extent. You cannot change everything, but things such as coloring will be easy eventually. For now, though, just picture yourself without your wings."

I sighed and did as he asked. After a few minutes of concentration, I heard him say, "Good job, Fala."

I opened my eyes once more and turned around to see my handiwork. I was disappointed. Most of my wings were still there, though I could see that quite a few of the feathers appeared to be missing. "I'm not even close."

"True, but most people could only make a feather or two disappear on their first try. To have made such a noticeable difference the first time is impressive."

This was supposed to be impressive? At this rate, Amahté would be healed before I could control my magic.

Still, after a few lessons, I could definitely appreciate my progress. I was able to hide my wings completely at will, and Osiris had moved on to teaching me some water spells.

"Water spells are the best type to learn," he explained, "because they can be used for anything. There are spells for the offensive and the defensive, for hurting and for healing. No other type of spell is so flexible."

I agreed to learn these types quickly. They would help me protect both myself and the ones I cared about, and to be able to heal people would be fantastic. I was eager to learn as much as I could as fast as I could.

Sometimes I would spend my spare time with Akori, but more often than not I was with Osiris. Akori was kind and supportive, but I could tell that his thoughts were with Amisi in the next room. Khenti had been taken care of—both he and Miu were gone for good. We wouldn't have to deal with them anymore. Set, on the other hand, was a different story.

"Can't you do *anything* to him, At?" I asked one day. It was ridiculous to me, this idea that he couldn't be touched. He had caused so much harm, and we could prove it beyond a shadow of a doubt.

"He is also a High God, Fala. As much as we do not like it, the human world needs him and his power. We will simply have to be more cautious in the future."

I frowned. I hated this—Set was the one responsible for my Mwt's death, and Amahté's pain, and I couldn't do a thing about it.

Osiris smiled gently, and patted me on the shoulder. "Do not worry, Fala. I know that this is hard for you. But I can assure you that this does not happen often—in fact, this is the first time since my childhood that Set has caught me so off my guard."

"Oh...that's good, I suppose..."

He nodded, and changed the topic. He knew it upset me.

Sitting with Amahté was frustrating. I could see him healing, and that made me feel better, but the idea that he might never wake up was...horrifying. Isis was keeping him alive with her magic. If his mind was gone, if she had to let him die...

Ugh. I didn't even want to think about it.

When I wasn't learning magic with Osiris, I tried to busy myself with other things, like helping Akori with his Ab's estate. Things were in shambles at the twins' home. With Khenti gone and Amahté still unconscious, *someone* had to be named heir to everything. Akori was the only one eligible, and now he was trying to organize the mess his Ab had left behind. I couldn't help but laugh a little; Khenti had sworn that Akori would never see a penny of that estate, and now he was running it.

He was doing a pretty good job, too—much better than his father. Khenti had apparently had a gambling problem, and he owed a lot to a lot of people. Akori sold off most of the impractical things that his Ab had commissioned—the battle-scene door was one of the first things to go—and was able to pay off all of Khenti's debt. Things were getting done more quickly, too, now that the servants were happier and actually being taken care of.

I wasn't able to do much—just put some papers in order. Still, anything was better than just sitting around waiting. I kept talking to Amahté, telling him what I was doing. Isis said that there was a good chance he could make out my voice, even if he didn't know what I was saying.

Osiris continued to stop by, but as the weeks turned into months he came by less and less. He didn't say anything, but I could see that he thought Amahté would never wake up. Akori didn't say anything, but he was starting to believe it, too. I tried to stay positive—I didn't want to give up on Amahté. It was hard, though, when Isis stopped answering when I asked if he would wake up soon.

That was why I was so relieved when his eyes fluttered

open for the first time.

At first I thought that I had imagined it, that it was wishful thinking. But when his eyelids fluttered a second time, I called for Isis.

"Amahté? Amahté, can you hear me?"

"Ngh...Fala?" He squinted up at me, just barely turning his head.

"I'm here, Amahté, I'm here. How do you feel?"

"...hurts..."

"I know, I'm sorry. Does it feel better than before?"

"Yeah...can' move m' legs..."

I felt my blood run cold. Was that something that could be fixed? Or was it too late? "Not even a little? Can you try to move a little for me?"

"...wanna sleep..."

"No, Amahté, you have to stay awake just a little while longer—" It was too late. He had already drifted off again.

"Fala? You called?"

Isis was here—could she wake him up again? "He was awake. Just now, he talked to me."

She rushed to the bedside, her hands already prepared for any healing she might have to do. "How long was he awake? Was he coherent? Did he know where he was?"

"Ah...just long enough for a few sentences, but he seemed to know what was going on. I don't know if he knew where he was, but he knew that it was me."

She nodded. "That is a good sign. The first

awakening is often most difficult for the body. Now he should come in and out of it more often. Then I can better ascertain what he needs, what is causing him the most pain and trouble…" She was off, mumbling to herself about what she could do next.

I left her to it—Akori deserved to know that his brother would be waking up soon, if only for a short while. And I could ask him what to do about his brother's legs; he was sure to know more about it than I did.

I found Amisi first, but that was alright. She would know where Akori was. "Amisi, can you take me to Akori? Amahté just woke up, and I want to let him know."

"Oh, goodness—he is this way, follow me!" I had to run to keep up with her as she led me through the hallways. How was it that she knew this place better than I did?

We ran into Osiris along the way—that was good, but I didn't really want to stop. I wanted to get to Akori and get then back to Amahté's side. I just called to him as we walked by, "Isis is with Amahté right now, he just woke up, we're going to get Akori."

"Wait, what—"

"I'm sorry, I can't wait!" I said over my shoulder. Amisi and I were already almost around the next corner. I could talk to Osiris later; I'm sure he would understand.

As we turned, Amisi almost ran into Akori—literally. I had to pull her back to keep them from both toppling to the ground. "Are you okay, Amisi? Is something wrong?"

"Akori, Fala said that Amahté is—" She cut herself

off, gasping. Amisi was definitely *not* an endurance runner.

"What? Amahté is what?!" Akori said, a look of sheer panic on his face. Oh, dear Ra, did he think something was wrong? He was such a worry wart, always jumping to the worst conclusions.

"Everything is fine, Akori," I said quickly. "I wanted to find you and tell you that Amahté woke up a few minutes ago. He even talked a little bit."

Akori's answering smile was blinding. "He is awake? He is okay?"

I nodded. "He fell back asleep, but Isis said that this is a great sign. She said he should be waking up again soon...I thought you should know."

He closed his eyes and took a deep breath, the smile still on his face. "I'm so happy," he said. "I thought...I was afraid that...but that doesn't matter now." He opened his eyes again and took Amisi's hand. "Can I see him?"

"Of course, Akori, you don't have to ask me. He's your brother."

"...Okay." Ah, he was so sweet. I was so glad to have a friend like him.

"Akori..." I didn't want to ruin it, but I didn't want him to be caught off guard. "You should know. When he woke up, he said...he said that he couldn't move his legs. I don't know if that's temporary or...not."

His smile faded a bit, but he said, "At least he is awake. That...that is better than nothing. If it is permanent...we will deal with that later."

"Come on, Akori," Amisi said softly. "Let us go see your brother." He nodded, and we headed off to see Amahté.

When we walked in, Isis was still there, and Amahté was awake once more. Amisi hung back a little—as she put it, Amahté "would want to see you two before me". Amahté looked at us for a moment, his eyes cloudy, and I was afraid that he didn't know who we were.

But then he smiled and said, "Hi, Fala. Hi, Akori. Sorry to worry you…"

Akori smiled. "That's okay, Amahté. I'm glad you are awake now."

"Me too…"

"Are his legs alright?" I asked Isis. "He said that he couldn't move them."

"That is perfectly fine," she said. "He has been unconscious for—nearly two months now, I do believe. The muscles must re-develop, especially with how much healing he had to undergo." I breathed a sigh of relief. Amahté might have to work at it, but he would be alright.

Things were noticeably better with Amahté awake. He still wasn't fully healed, and he tended to drift off in the middle of things, but we knew that he would be alright. Isis stopped by every day still, but the visits became shorter and shorter.

Akori was the one who seemed most different. Even when he had inherited the estate, he was still constantly worrying about his brother. Now that both his Ab and the worry were out of the way, he was so much more confident. Amisi joked that he was a totally different person from the one she had first met. It was strange, but it was nice to see him so comfortable in his own skin.

I was with Amahté most of the time, helping him sit up at first, and later helping him to walk. Isis had said that he might have to learn to walk again because his legs were so damaged. We had to get on that right away, something that didn't go very well at first.

"I hate this!" Amahté said one day, flopping back in defeat. His voice was rougher now, not smooth like it had been when I first met him. Isis said it was because there had been damage to his throat that she wasn't able to heal fully. I wouldn't tell Amahté, because it would upset him, but…I liked it.

"You can do it, Amahté. Just one more try." I reached over to grab his arm and help him up, but he shook me off.

"What's the point? I can't walk properly, I'll probably never be able to run or fight ever again. I'm useless!"

I sighed and sat down beside him. At least he hadn't been awake for the worst of it. If he felt like this now, I couldn't imagine how he would feel if he had been awake when he had first been hurt. He would have been horrified at having to be moved and treated and even bathed by someone else. True, he was still healing, but most of his skin had grown back, at least.

"…Fala?"

"Yes?"

"What would you do if I said I was giving up?"

"I'd say that you'll be able to do it if you keep trying. Just don't give up."

"What if I still said no?"

"Then I'd smack you and make you get up and do your exercises." He stared at me. Well, no one could accuse me of being dishonest.

"…Let's go, then." I smiled, and helped him back to his feet to keep working. Slowly but surely, Amahté was regaining the use of his legs.

With the danger gone, Amahté and I could talk about what we really wanted. We weren't rushing this time; we didn't have to. We could take our time. Not that we had much of a choice but to wait, with Amahté still recovering.

I couldn't wait to get back to Egypt. Osiris had promised not to stop us, something that really helped me. And one day, he pulled me aside.

"I would like to give you something, Fala," he said.

"Oh, no, At, I don't need anything."

He rolled his eyes. "Yes, you do. I believe that in the midst of all this you have forgotten one very important thing." I thought about it for a moment, but nothing came to mind. When I finally gave up and shrugged, he laughed and said, "A house, Fala. You are forgetting that you need a house."

How could I forget that? I couldn't go back home— people would be convinced, now more than ever, that I was some evil being. I would have to move to somewhere entirely new. "Oh, Ra…will you help me find one, At?"

"I will do better than that." He took my arm gently and, with a quick incantation, we were both back in Egypt. I cringed, and immediately grabbed my wings self-consciously. "Do not worry, Fala. No one can see us."

Oh. The twins had had the same problem, but I had forgotten about that completely. "Are we here to look at a house…?"

Osiris pulled me over to a nearby house and opened the door, gesturing me to go inside. I went in slowly. What if I didn't like it? Would I hurt his feelings?

As I looked around, though, I realized that wasn't going to be a problem. This was the house of my dreams!

"You'll love it, Amahté, it's fantastic," I said later.

"How big is it?"

"It's practically a palace! Well, maybe not that big, but it certainly has more than enough rooms. There is a kitchen, and two lounging rooms, and a room for us plus three more. And the garden is beautiful!"

"Where is it?"

"In Abydos. Isn't that perfect? We were going to look there anyway?"

"Do we really need that much space? It's only going to be the two of us, with Akori and Amisi staying at home."

"It's only the two of us *now*. We need space for when Akori and Amisi come to visit—I am *not* just sticking them on the floor. And besides," I added more quietly, "Later on, once we're settled in…we'll need room for the little ones."

Amahté jerked back and nearly fell out of the bed. "Little ones?" he squeaked. "When? We're not even married!"

"Well I didn't mean right now!" I said, pulling him back to the center of the bed. "I meant later, after we're married, after we're settled. I wouldn't even mind waiting a few years, just…I think it's something to keep in mind."

"Oh…" He sighed in relief and sat back. "Okay. …Good point. Ra, don't scare me like that!"

I rolled my eyes. "Now that you're done overreacting, is there anything else you want to know about the house?"

"What about the servants' quarters? How were they?"

I bit my lip. "Those…were nice." I was still reluctant to have servants around. I had always been self-sufficient, even when I was staying with the twins. It seemed odd to change that now, but with a house that big, there was no way I could do it on my own. "Can we take Kemreit with us? She's back at Khe-Akori's estate."

I saw Amahté flinch. I'd told him what happened with Khenti. He would have heard it from the servants anyway— somehow they knew *everything* about *everyone*. Of course he didn't approve, but…it was still his Ab. I tried not to mention him when I could get away with it. "Who is Kemreit?"

"She lived in the same village as I did. She's so nice, and she's a really hard worker." I wanted to get to know her better. If she was good enough to be counted on when I only kind of knew her, then she was certainly good enough to come and live with us. I was sure that she missed Egypt as much as I did.

"She can come…I don't mind. I know a few other servants that can be trusted…I'll talk to Akori about it…" He was drifting off again. The medicine Isis was giving him tended to do that.

"Go to sleep, Amahté," I said softly. "I'll still be here when you wake up." He nodded once, and before long he was asleep.

"How is he?"

"He's fine," I said without turning. I knew it was just Osiris. "He just fell asleep, but he has been able to stay awake for much longer."

"That is good."

I didn't say anything more. One of the first things that I had learned about Osiris was that he was a man of few words. If he wanted to say something, then he would, but otherwise making conversation was impossible. I could tell he wanted to say something, but he would say it in his own time.

"Fala…"

I moved to face him. He looked almost…guilty. "Yes?"

"I…I told your Mwt what had happened. She would like to speak with you."

I opened my mouth, then closed it again and bit my lip. I would love to see my Mwt, but… "I promised Amahté that I would be here when he woke up."

"It will be quick. Perhaps not there, but in this world it will be only a moment that has passed."

"…Okay." Amahté wouldn't mind. If it was only a moment here it was fine; there was no way that he would wake up that quickly. I stood to meet Osiris and took his arm. The horrible darkness came up, and this time I was proud to say that I didn't flinch back. It was still oppressive, but somehow it didn't seem as bad as before. Maybe because I was learning to control my magic.

We finally landed, and this time I didn't hesitate—I ran straight to the cottage where I could see my Mwt in the window.

"Fala! Sweetie!" I got the same warm hug as last time; it was nice. The twins were kind and caring, but they certainly couldn't match a Mwt's love.

"Hey, Mut. How are you?"

She smiled brightly. "I am fine, Fala. Same as ever." The smile faded from her face, though, and she continued, "I am worried about you."

Ugh, what had Osiris told her? I just shrugged. "Oh no, I'm okay. I... Amahté is the one to be worried about."

"Osiris said that you were hurt too. How is your leg? How is your shoulder?"

"They are *fine*, Mut. See?" I moved my arm back and forth, then bent my knee to show that I was all healed. Why would Osiris make her worry like that? "I'm not hurt anymore."

Mut sighed. "Come on, baby girl. Sit down." I let her lead me to a chair, sitting without saying a word. "Fala, I know that Amahté is the one still healing. Osiris told me that. But just because you are not hurt *physically* does not mean that you are fine. Please, be honest with me."

I took a deep, shuddering breath. I didn't want to do this right now; I shouldn't have come. "I…things are fine *now*. I was afraid that I was going to lose Amahté for the longest time, but now Isis says that he is getting better every day. He will be alright soon, and we can have our home."

She smiled back at me. "Of course, Fala. I just want to make sure that you are taking care of yourself. This is not going to be worth it if you do not take care of your own well-being."

I shrugged it off, although I knew it was true. The danger was over now, and we could all focus on recovering. "Really, Mut. Things are fine now. I know everything will be okay." That seemed to make her feel at least a little bit better.

She still looked like she didn't believe me. "If you say so, baby girl. But if you ever need to talk, I am here. I am sure that Osiris will bring you. Now. You and Amahté are very close, yes?"

"Yes, we're going to be moving into one house as soon as he is well enough."

"So when do I get little grandchildren?"

I stared at her. Sure, I had said we needed room for children, but I had meant in a few *years*. "…Maybe in two or three years?"

She pouted. "Well, that is not very fair. I would love to see you have children. And I know that Osiris has said he would love to have a little granddaughter to spoil."

When I looked over at Osiris, he pointedly looked in

the opposite direction. "Has he, now?"

"Yes."

"Mwt, I love you, but there are definitely not any children in the immediate future."

"Oh, alright," she sighed. "You will let me know though, will you not?"

"Of course, Mut." I shifted in my seat a little. I was getting antsy being away from Amahté.

I stood to leave, but she grabbed my arm and pulled me down again. "Wait, sweetie, perhaps we could just chat a bit?"

"Any other time, Mut, I would love to, but I really need to be going. I want to get back to Amahté and take care of him." She glanced at Osiris, but still held my arm. "I promise that I will come back soon to see you, alright? But I have to go now."

Reluctantly, she pulled her arm back. "...Alright, Fala. I will see you soon. I love you."

"I love you too," I said softly. Now I felt badly for leaving her. I knew she wasn't alone, but it seemed as though she really wanted me to stay.

Osiris came over and placed a hand on my other arm. "It is alright, Teanna. I will bring her back soon."

My Mwt nodded and let go of my arm reluctantly. I bent down to give her a quick hug before holding on to Osiris. He seemed a little nervous—not scared-nervous, but nervous like he was keeping a secret.

"Is something going on?" I asked as we hurtled

through the darkness. "You and Mut were acting a little...off."

He smiled at me awkwardly. "We were simply...expecting you to stay longer."

"Why does it matter?"

He didn't answer, and just as he stopped we arrived right outside of Amahté's room. I sighed and went in—I really didn't care either way. It apparently wasn't my business.

"Hi, Amahté, I'm back—OH RA WHERE IS HE?"

Amahté was gone! His bed was empty, his clothes were gone. Had Isis moved him? We hadn't been gone that long, and she wouldn't move without telling me, right?

"Fala, please, perhaps you could just calm down—"

"Calm down? Calm *down?!*" Amahté was missing, and Osiris wanted me to be calm? He was injured still, and if he pushed himself too hard, who knew what that would do to his recovery?

"Fala, I am sure that there is a reason for his not being here," Osiris said gently.

I took a deep breath. "Okay, okay, reason. Right. I have to go find Isis." If there *was* a reason that he had been moved, then she would be able to tell me. He wouldn't have been moved without her knowledge or her orders, right?

I didn't wait to hear Osiris approve of my plan. I just headed off, hoping that I would run into someone— anyone—along the way. Isis had always been nearby at first, but as Amahté had gotten better, she became harder and harder to find.

"Isis," I called. "Isis!"

"Is there something wrong, Miss Fala?"

I nearly jumped out of my own skin. I'd been looking for her, it's true, but I still couldn't figure out how she just appeared out of *nowhere* like this. Shaking my head, I said, "Isis, did you move Amahté? Or tell one of the assistants to have him moved?"

She frowned. "No, I did no such thing. He is not in his bed?"

My heart sank. Where could he be? "He's not even in his *room*."

"Oh, goodness. I hope he did not go too far; he really should not be moving around very much yet."

Well, that didn't help my nerves! Ra, Amahté was such an idiot sometimes—why couldn't he just wait until he was healed? He just had to push everything.

"Thank you, Isis. Please let me know if you see him anywhere." She nodded, and I headed off at a run. Where could he be?

My pace slowed as I realized something awful. What if Set had sent someone else? Someone to finish what his last assassin had started?

I took off even faster than before, looking behind every door and turning my head to look at every corner. I couldn't search fast enough—literally. Whether he was on his own or not, Amahté was probably moving around at the same time I was. We could be passing each other in parallel hallways and not even know it.

"Oh Amahté, why couldn't you just stay in your room?" This was not okay. I was really starting to panic now; my heart was hammering so hard that I felt like it was going to fly out of my chest. "Oh, dear Ra, please let him be safe," I prayed, a small sob ripping its way out of my mouth. No! I couldn't cry now, I hadn't cried this whole time...

But that was part of the problem. I hadn't cried throughout this whole damned thing. I'd been trying too hard to keep things together for Akori, and now that one sob had broken free the rest followed. I stopped and slid down against the wall. This couldn't be happening. We had been through so much together, and just when things were finally going to be alright, Amahté had to go missing again.

"No..." I did my best to dry my eyes and staggered to my feet. Crying wouldn't find him. I had to get up and move.

"Fala?"

I turned to Akori and took a deep, shuddering breath. "Akori, Amahté is missing," I said weakly.

"I know, Isis told me. That is how I found you. He is not really missing, do you know that?"

I stared at him. "Akori," I said slowly, a few tears still trickling, "why would no one tell me if Amahté was moved?" That was not alright. Everyone knew how much I was worried about him, even if no one said anything, so why would this be kept a secret?

Akori fidgeted a little bit. "Well...Lord Osiris and your Mwt were meant to keep you away longer. We did not mean for you to panic."

"You…" I paused and took a deep breath, wiping the last few tears from my cheeks before I continued. "Were you all in on this?"

"Well…"

"Akori." I stepped away from the wall, closer to him. My heart was still pounding. If they were all in this together, then I would probably be more relieved than angry. That would mean Amahté was safe.

"Everyone except for Isis knew. Please, Fala, I promised Amahté that I would not tell you. He will tell you everything when he returns, but for now I need you to trust me." He reached his hand out to me. "Let us go back to Amahté's room. That is where he is expecting you to be when he gets back."

I put my head in my hands and took a deep, shaky breath. I wasn't sure if I was more angry with everyone for playing me like this or more relieved that Amahté was alright. Maybe my Mwt was right; maybe I did need a break.

After a moment, I stood up and took Akori's hand. "When your brother gets back, Akori, I'm going to be so mad at you."

He smiled back at me. "I truly doubt that, Fala."

"Mmfrglshr…" Stupid Akori and his stupid riddles.

I had to lean on him for most of the way back. I hadn't totally gotten my legs back from my little breakdown—it felt like that had been happening more and more lately. Amahté and I really needed a break. I couldn't wait to get to that house in Abydos…

When we arrived, Akori sat me down on Amahté's bed. I was biting my nails, and if I didn't stop soon I would be biting my fingers instead of my nails. The fact that Amahté had gotten up and away on his own was encouraging, but if Isis didn't know that he was moving around that meant she hadn't given him permission. I hoped he didn't push himself too hard…

"Fala, please do not worry," Akori pleaded.

"Aha, yeah, not worrying. Thanks, Akori, that's so helpful."

He sighed and rubbed his forearm. "I am sorry, Fala. I wish I could tell you more. …We had thought that you would stay longer with your Mwt."

"I know," I said, rolling my eyes. "You said that already. I don't mean to take it out on you." I was mad at him, but that really wasn't fair. Amahté could ask Akori to kill someone and he would; he would do anything for his brother without a second thought. Of course he wouldn't think twice about doing this.

I flopped back against the bed and covered my eyes. Maybe I could just sleep until Amahté got here. That probably wouldn't be long now—I had spent quite a while running around trying to find him.

Akori refused to leave the room. I asked him a few times if he wanted to go find Amisi, but he seemed to feel like he had to stay. He didn't get the hint that I wanted to be alone right now to collect myself. I didn't even know what I was going to say to Amahté when he got back; part of me wanted to yell at him for going missing, part of me wanted to hug him, and part of me wanted to go missing as payback.

In the end, though, I decided to just wait and talk to him about it. He was alive, and soon enough, we would be able to have a quiet life. I almost laughed out loud at that; who would have guessed that I would make it through all this to get back to *normal*? That would take some adjusting…

I must have fallen asleep without realizing it, because the next thing I knew, someone was shaking me.

"Fala? Come on, you were supposed to be awake when I got back." Oh, Amahté was back.

I groaned and pushed him off a little. "Amahté, you were the one who disappeared in the first place."

"Hey, it was with good intentions. I'm sure that you will enjoy this just as much as I will. If you decide to sit up, that is."

"Fine," I huffed playfully, sitting up and swinging my legs over the side of the bed. "Where were you, exactly?"

Amahté rolled his eyes and stood up, taking my hands. "I had to go back to the estate. I wanted to get ahold of something in particular. It's been waiting for a while, actually." He paused to pull me up, and as he did, he slipped something on my wrist.

I looked down and saw that it was a beautiful golden bracelet, made with small sapphires and lapus lazuli around the edges. "It's beautiful, Amahté."

"I'm glad you think so," he smiled, "because I'm asking you to be my wife."

I stared at him, open-mouthed. "What?"

"I want to marry you, Fala. I would love for you to be my wife, my partner, my equal—" He paused to kiss me on the cheek, and murmured, "my soulmate."

"Amahté..." He was so romantic, even if he didn't want to admit it. It was really cute. "I would love that, Amahté."

"Really?"

"No, I just said that to make you feel better. Of *course*, really."

He laughed nervously, and rubbed his hand behind his head. "Oh, Ra, thank goodness. I was afraid you were going to be so mad at me for disappearing that you would say no..."

I sighed and hugged him tightly. "I *am* mad at you. You're still injured, you know. My heart almost stopped when I came back and you were gone. Speaking of which," I added, "*you* need to get back to bed."

As I helped him back to lie down, he grumbled, "It doesn't matter anyway. I'm going to be killed now matter what."

"Why?" I asked him, startled.

"I have to tell your Ab you said yes."

I just laughed and shook my head.

Epilogue
—Ten Years Later

"So how have you been, Akori?" I asked.

He smiled and leaned back, stretching his arms behind his head. "Fine. Afrikaisi took her first steps the other day, and she did pretty well until Ashai pushed her over—he seems to like picking on her."

"How are the triplets? Still troublesome?"

"Oh, gods yes," Akori laughed. "Akhom seems to be the mastermind of the group, though; Akana and Akorit seem to just follow him around. Aloli follows them, too, but I think she is only making sure that the girls do not get in too much trouble."

I shook my head. How he managed all of those children was beyond me—I was happy with three, thank you very much. "And you left Amisi alone with them?"

"Mkit is with her, and so is Biti. They are the best assistants available, and they know to call me the minute something goes wrong."

"I'm surprised you left her alone, with how close the baby is to being born."

He blushed. "Well…Amisi actually threatened me. She said that she could tell I wanted to be here, and she demanded that I come. She is fine, really, but Isis did not want her traveling. She is on bed-rest right now until little Amanit is born."

I laughed. "Who would have thought you would be the one with the biggest family?" He shrugged and I added, "Are you going to have more after this, or do you think that seven is going to be enough?"

"Well, seven *is* a lucky number, you know. And also, I think that Amisi is going to hurt me if I say that I would like more."

"That's probably true, actually," I told him.

"And *you* should not be talking about surprises, Fala. I never would have imagined that you would be the one staying home."

"I still *work*, you know. And when we tried leaving Amahté in charge of the house he almost burned it down," I said, though I knew he was joking. Akori knew what I did for a living; I helped organize ways to give orphans jobs. Good ones, where I knew they would be treated well. That mostly involved bringing them to work as servants, but that was better than living in the streets.

"So how is—"

"Mo-om! Nebi was hiding in my room again!!"

"No, I wasn't, I wasn't, it's because she stole my ball!"

I sighed. It seemed like the twins couldn't go a single day without fighting. "Both of you, come in here. You're going to wake the baby."

Nané and Nebi shuffled into the room looking guilty. "Hello, Uncle Akori," they mumbled.

Akori smiled. "Hello, Nané. Hello, Nebi. You are not making trouble for your Mwt, are you?"

"No, Uncle Akori."

I let the corner of my mouth quirk upwards into a little smile. "Well, not for me. They love making trouble for their Ab, though, because he's wrapped around their little fingers."

"When *is* At getting home?" Nané piped up. Ah, ever the At's little girl.

"He should be home soon. In the meantime, why don't you two tell me what was going on?" When both of them began to babble at once, I held up my hands and said, "One at a time, one at a time. Nané first."

"I walked into my room and he was digging under my bed. That's not fair, if I can't go in his room then he shouldn't be able to go into mine—"

"Okay, Nané. Nebi, were you under her bed?"

"Yeah, but only because she took my ball. It's under her bed right now, I saw it."

Oh, Ra, what was I going to do with these two? "Nané, did you take Nebi's ball?"

"Well, it depends what you mean by 'take'—" I looked at her and frowned, and she cut herself off. "...Yes, I took the ball."

"Alright. Nané, give Nebi his ball back. Nebi, don't go

digging in your sister's room. If she takes something, come to me."

"Yes, Mut," they replied in unison.

"And both of you are grounded for a week. No friends, no staying out past sunset. Understand?"

"Wait, Mut—"

"Tomorrow would be better—"

"Uncle Akori hasn't been here in forever—"

"Alright, alright," I said, holding my hands up. They were right; this was Akori's first visit in almost eight months. "Starting tomorrow, you're both grounded."

"Okay," they chorused, and ran off.

"Is that not a bit harsh, Fala?" Akori asked. "I know that they need to learn, but..."

I rolled my eyes. "If this were the first time, I would let it go. But this is the fourth time this week that this same thing has happened."

"Ah."

"Yes. Ah."

"Fala?" Oh, Amahté was home. "I'm back."

"In here, Amahté! Guess who came to visit?"

"Who?" he asked as he rounded the corner. "Akori! Where have you been?"

Akori laughed and stood to hug his brother. "I am sorry, I was busy. I can only stay the night, though."

"That's alright, I'm just glad to see you!" Off in a back room, there was a faint cry. "Oh, the baby. Can Kemreit get her?"

"The servants all retired early today. I asked them to give us some privacy."

"Okay. I'll be right back then...

"No, I'll get her, Amahté. Visit with your brother."

"Are you sure?"

"Yes, it's fine." I wasn't giving him a choice; I was already halfway out of the room. I knew how much Amahté missed his brother. And besides, the baby was probably hungry. "Hey, sweetie," I whispered as I entered her room. "How are you?"

Little Teanna stared back up at me, waving her little arms. She had slept for a long time today. I picked her up and settled her on my hip. She was almost a year old—she should be walking soon, but she wasn't quite there yet.

By the time I had gotten her fed and taken her back to the living room, everyone had settled in. The twins were sitting on either side of Akori, looking up in adoration as he told them a story. Amahté was standing right across from his brother, smiling.

"Hey," I said quietly, coming up beside him. "Everything settled down?"

"Yeah," he said, giving me a chaste kiss on the lips.

"Ew!"

"Mut and At are being gross!"

I rolled my eyes, and then leaned over to give Amahté a longer kiss. Hey, parents have to get their kicks in any way they can, right?

Nané and Nebi stuck their tongues out, and Akori

went back to telling his story. I leaned my head against Amahté's shoulder, and settled Teanna more comfortably against my chest.

I looked out at my happy little family and reached up, almost unconsciously, to finger the amulet that had given it all.

- The End.

Acknowledgements:

I want to thank my family for all their support, and I want to thank my friends for helping me with my countless requests for editing. I especially want to thank Amanda, who encouraged me to write this book in the first place, and Kat, who designed and drew the cover art.

I'm also so grateful to Mr. Pogodzinski for helping me throughout this entire process and for agreeing to publish me in the first place.

Finally, I want to say thank you to anyone and everyone who buys this book. I sincerely hope that you will enjoy it!

www.ingramcontent.com/pod-product-compliance
Lightning Source LLC
Chambersburg PA
CBHW070329260626
47160CB00003B/990